ABOVE THE SUMMIT

A Novel

by

Bill Seery

Chapter 1

QUIET DISQUIET

Mt. Whitney, California
June 2
9:20 a.m. (PDT)

"This mountain has something different for everyone who comes here." Jason Greer pondered the words of his late friend, Jay Gibbons, as he stepped onto the summit of Mt. Whitney and gazed over the eastern cliff. A fellow ranger with the U.S. Forest Service, Jay had lost his life fighting a large forest fire the previous summer. Today, twelve months later, Jason was serving as a guide for a small group of hikers. Since he had reached the top first, he had a few minutes to enjoy the solitude as he waited for them to catch up.

One hundred yards down the trail the four other members of his party plodded wearily upward. Jason watched the tiny figures grow more distinct as they neared the top. While the blue sky above was bright and cloudless, the air was chilly —the kind of day on the summit where you can be cold and get sunburned at the same time.

At long last, their final steps to the top were met by the

Many thanks to my amazing wife, Marcie, my family, and to all those
who encouraged, supported, and persevered with me in this venture.

Above the Summit

Web addresses:
www.abovethesummit.info
www.bowerbrokersseries.info

Primary editing by Sarah Hood

Cover design by Stephen Yeakley
Cover image is under license.

Above the Summit is a work of fiction. Similarities to real places, people, organizations and some aspects of science have been altered to enhance the story, which is, again, fictitious.

ISBN 979-8-9888443-0-3

Library of Congress Control Number: 2023914112

Printed in the United States of America

triumphant voice of their leader: "Congratulations, ladies and gentlemen, you have peaked!"

A weathered brass survey marker, fixed on the highest granite boulder, confirmed their arrival at the official summit, where the view was spectacular. The party had camped at a lower altitude the night before, continuing the climb before dawn. Now, at 14,505 feet above sea level, everyone but Jason felt the queasy tug of altitude sickness. And even though Jason was fully acclimated, for the last few months, he had been feeling his own queasiness for reasons other than elevation. In fact, for him, the altitude helped.

For the other members of his party, this achievement was a first. Two women in the group were friends and marked it as their highest mountain peak on a list of other personal challenges. The other two hikers were tech students from Pomona on summer break.

Amid groans, grumbles, and intermittent swearing, the apprentice mountaineers shed their packs and stumbled clumsily over each other. Most of their inelegance was from simple fatigue after an arduous morning of walking uphill. The rest was an overwhelming sense of awe at the surrounding scenery.

"Jason," said one of the students, wheezing, "how can you climb this mountain and still be fresh? It's not even fair."

"Practice, Chet. Practice," said Jason. "I guess you could say I've been up here a lot."

A lot was true. He repeated this climb whenever he got the chance, most often as a guide, like today. Other times, he fit it into various assignments as a ranger.

"So, do you do it for the challenge?" Chet asked.

"Not exactly. It's just something I do," he said. "I like to come up here to see if the world is still out there."

Chet and his friend, Nate, laughed, not realizing he was serious.

For Jason, out there meant far away from here. The summit was like a window to the world outside, through which he could see and assure himself again that the world beyond was still . . . out there.

Nate continued the joke. "Well, nothin' to worry about then. Looks like it's still there."

"Yep. So far, so good," Jason replied.

During the last few years, Jason's life had been going in a good direction. At the age of twenty-nine, he had a career he wanted to keep, a place to live that he liked, and even a cabin of his own. It was a world he wanted. He loved beauty, nature, and the challenge of a climb. He could hunt, fish, and survive in the wilderness—perhaps indefinitely. During his fairly new career as a ranger, he had also picked up basic firefighting and, for him, the adventure of rescuing people who were lost or in danger was a rush. Each year, there were enough of those situations for him to stay busy. Things were going so remarkably well—it was making him more nervous every day.

Generally, Jason was not a fearful or negative person. However, there had been times in his life when he sensed things he could not prove in the moment. Most disturbing of these was when he sensed disaster just before his parents died in a plane crash.

Recently a similar angst and apprehension had surfaced within him that he could not explain. In addition to that, strange things were happening at his residence—things that did not make sense.

So, ironically, at this most positive time in his life, Jason was distracted by a subjective, nameless threat. A solitary lookout on an ancient city wall might have felt the same angst, watching in the night for the intrusion of an enemy. Perhaps it was just a feeling. However, irrational as it was, he returned here to look—frequently, like checking to see if the door is locked for the fifth or sixth time before going to bed. It helped. But still, he thought now, *whatever this is, I hope it stays out there.*

Chapter 2

WATER TIL WINTER

Mt. Whitney, California
June 2
9:30 a.m. (PDT)

Individually and together, the hikers surveyed and explored their newly-claimed territory. As they gazed downward, thousands of feet toward the base of the cliffs, they saw their stark, jagged surroundings fade to a gentler texture below. Spring had done its job, jump-starting new growth for summer to take over before the water became ice again. In front of them was the most vibrant version of the canyon.

"When the weather changes, lightning strikes here sometimes," said Jason. "Lucky for us it's a clear day."

"Is that why this shack was put here?" Chet was pointing toward a small stone building standing alone just below the highest point.

"Not as much for lightning as for shelter in a storm. Winter is not as friendly as what we see today."

Having explored the barren top of the mountain and photographed 360 degrees of scenery, the whole group clustered together and stood gazing off the steepest cliff.

Jason said, "Right now we are at the highest point in the lower forty-eight states of the U.S. One hundred miles that way is Death Valley, which is the lowest point. About eighty miles that way is the entrance to the China Lake Naval Weapons Center, where they test all the new stuff they don't tell you about."

One of the two women was looking down at something in the canyon and said, "That looks like a little lake down there."

Jason answered, "You're right, Beth. Beautiful, isn't it? All summer long, snow melts and flows down from up here. The water collects in that basin," Jason pointed to the lake below, "which is just a few hundred yards across, turning it into a delicate blue lake. We should be able to see other ones like it as well. Eventually, the lake overflows so some of that water escapes and continues down the slope. As it falls, it picks up speed and power, and eventually, it morphs into a loud, rushing creek winding through the forest. It's Lone Pine Creek, where we started hiking yesterday. Right there. See it?"

Everyone leaned out to try to follow where he pointed.

"Eh, no—er, yes. There."

"Where?"

"Over to the right and further out."

"Oh, yeah. Okay."

"Careful guys—this is a cliff, okay?" said Beth's friend, Patrice.

Jason continued, "You can't see the lower forest very well from here, though."

"Check it out, guys!" A voice from behind them was accompanied by a high-pitched whirring sound. Turning, they saw Nate holding a remote control with a tablet video screen attached.

At his feet, a small, empty black case lay open and, rising very quickly from about eye level, a black drone with silver trim soared above them all. It moved off the cliff and outward toward the open canyon.

Everyone stepped back and clustered behind Nate to see the screen. It was a bird's-eye view. The drone made its way far down between two massive granite cliffs with a forest between them, the one Jason had just been talking about. As it flew lower, thirty or so dark brown cabin roofs became visible through the treetops, sprinkled over the forest area. Casual, intermittent smoke signals floated up from chimneys and campground fires. Since they had all been there the previous day, they recognized it as the Mt. Whitney Portal area, complete with campsites, a creek, picnic tables, and parking for campers.

Below the Portal area, they could see the one road connecting it with the outside world winding down through an area known as the Alabama Hills. For years, this had been a popular site for making movies. At the top end of that road, above the campground, was a store and the trailhead, where they had begun their hike.

"Uh-oh," said Nate.

"Battery?" asked Chet.

"Yep. I won't be able to get the drone to climb all the way back up here. We're talking at least five thousand feet up from there. Going down was a lot less work for it."

Looking at the screen over Nate's shoulder, Jason said, "Fly around the campground and look for an RV with what looks like a living room of furniture next to it outside and a solar panel at the front." He paused. "That's it. Land it on that guy's roof. He's the camp host, Logan Faris. He'll take care of it. We can get it from him on the way out."

"Yes! Done," said Nate.

They all cheered.

"I have a question," said Chet. "What if we come back here during the winter?"

Jason replied, "Can't—er, not usually. The roads are closed, covered with a lot of feet of snow. There is no real place to stay."

"What about your place?"

"What do you mean?"

"Someone said you stay here during the winter."

"Yeah, I heard there was a rumor like that." Changing the topic, Jason said, "Really, you don't want to be here in winter. It may be compelling to think about right now when conditions are great, but that changes quickly."

Jason went on, explaining in great detail about the passage from autumn to winter, how it starts one silent night, early in November, when individual snowflakes settle lightly on tree branches and trails like miniature works of art. Quiet and serene, the snowfall is a lovely adornment—at first. Then, it becomes relentless. Storms roll in and, by late December, everything is sealed under a frozen canvas of white. Anyone lingering in the forest soon discovers that survival is the highest priority as they wait out the stubborn, cold winter. There is no stopping these quiet, unrelenting forces of nature.

"When you get back to the trailhead, go over to the little store by the pond," Jason added. "Greg, the old guy in charge, has lived on and around this mountain since he was twenty and has a lot to say about winter. He'll tell you how he used to trudge up to where the store is on snowshoes during winter, but only for a day at a time from where the road was closed because of the snow. Get him to tell you some of the stories of people who underestimated the harsh winter here and either barely made it or their bodies were discovered in the spring when the snow melted."

Beth said, "That sounds fine, Jason, but right now we better think about getting back down the trail before the sun sets."

Beth was right. Even though the small band of explorers had chosen the best time of year for their quest, today they needed to get back—hopefully before dark.

For Jason, however, talking about winter was making him more uneasy than the thought of getting back after dark. He wondered, *Could it be this winter?*

Chapter 3

HATING WAITING

China Lake, California
June 2
3:00 p.m. (PDT)

Air Force Lieutenant Colonel Alexander Larson stepped into the elevator, turned around, and pressed the button marked "-4B." As the two stainless steel doors rumbled across the opening in front of him, touching in the middle, he saw his own image frowning back—forty-three-year-old Caucasian male, six feet, two inches, trim, with light blond hair and mustache. He had just gotten his hair cut; although each time he did, there was less to bother with. On his lapel was an oak leaf patch, signifying his rank, along with a variety of other designations for his years of service.

Alex had followed a family military tradition like his adoptive father, John; had even ended up outranking the elder Larson. Alex's status was well-earned with over twenty-one years of service. Most of it had been as a combat fighter pilot, including two tours in Iraq and a fairly large collection of discrete missions which he could not discuss. His pilot call sign, "Savage One," accurately reflected his aggressiveness and focus during combat. Alex's assignments had required both intellect and skill and because some of these operations were unique in character, briefings for them tended to be much longer and more detailed than they were "brief." Consequently, Alex was accustomed to—and insisted upon—being well-informed, not only about the immediate tactical objectives of a mission but on the broader strategic purpose. Perhaps he felt more entitled than he should have. However, he had earned a high degree of respect among his peers because he had always been more than a technician carrying out orders. Instead, he was a vital part of command.

Alex had no serious aspirations for a promotion to a higher rank. He was concerned that the higher in rank he was, the less he would be able to fly in combat situations because he would become a different sort of asset. Meanwhile, whenever he could not be privy to top intelligence, it annoyed him greatly. Today he was annoyed—greatly.

Damn Connor thinks he's in charge of the entire Air Force. Something flew up his butt after he got his precious brigadier status. Now he sits behind his brick wall general's desk withholding information. Thoughts like these were not rare for Alex. He had sense enough to keep them inside his head—though, when the time was right, he was not afraid to speak his mind.

From his experience in combat, he had become exceptionally good at spotting discrepancies, like the day he and now Brigadier General Brian Connor, once his wingman and friend, had been flying low over the desert in Iraq. A rippled pattern in the sand caught his eye as they sped past. It didn't look quite right. Glancing back, he spotted smoke and the flames of two surface-to-air missiles rising toward them from behind a camouflage cover. His keen early perception and decisiveness gave him the few seconds they needed to escape and survive.

Now, this skill was coming in handy for a peacetime application. During the last few months, since his transfer to China Lake, something had not looked quite right. Certain people, with whom he had worked closely in the past, seemed to be giving subtle messages or, perhaps, non-messages—the kind that are obvious but deniable. Brian Connor was one of these people. Like yesterday. Alex had received two contradicting emails. One was from the office of Two-Star General Johnathan Bundy and the other from Brian Connor's administrative assistant. Together, they boiled down to a deniable he said-she said.

He said, "Request your presence in General Connor's office for a preliminary intel briefing with officers at 1500 hours. We would like your perspective on a possible mission. Please confirm."

As soon as he got it, Alex sent a confirmation reply.

A few minutes later, she, Connor's administrative assistant, wrote, "General Connor would like you to attend an intelligence briefing in his office tomorrow at 1530 hours."

Apparently, thought Alex, *Bundy wants me there for the whole briefing, but Connor wants me there late. Wouldn't be the first time. What is it with his power hangup?*

Sometimes punctuality goes both ways—especially when the stakes are high, and trust is low. Alex could decide to be punctual with Connor and offend Bundy, a higher-ranking officer; or he could be punctual with Bundy and have Connor working against him. He did not want to lose the opportunity for a new assignment from Bundy. Neither did he want Connor controlling him. So, rather than checking to verify the time in case there was a mistake, he decided to show up at 1500 hours as he had confirmed—despite his distrust of Connor. This way, at least he could learn something from Connor's response.

At 1500 hours, he arrived at Connor's office and told his administrative assistant that he was there for the briefing. "I'm so sorry, sir," she said, "but General Connor just called and said he had to postpone your briefing. He asked me to express his sincere apologies but that it was unavoidable. He said he will contact you as soon as they are ready to get started again."

Alex thanked her politely and walked toward the small lunchroom at the end of the hallway.

'Sincere apologies.' Not likely, he thought as he took a bite of a stale brownie from a vending machine, then threw the rest of it away.

Though he was trained for war, he never wished for it. However, with all its horrors, war felt almost preferable to petty politicking. At least in war, hostilities are declared and open. The fact that you are trying to beat your enemy is no secret.

For Alex, integrity was a big deal. A lot of good could be accomplished with integrity and a noble purpose. He was patriotic at heart, believing that tyranny is evil, and that strength should be used to protect and defend people from it. From a military perspective, he had always tended to ignore anything directly political. But for a while now, the issue of national integrity had been more concerning to him as he observed the political scene, mostly out of the corner of one eye. Alex had been back in the States for over four months, but the more he saw how people were acting in the culture, the more he knew he was out of his element. All he knew for sure was that his reassignment had come from "very high up." But he kept asking himself, Why would they send me here, to some weapons testing facility in the middle of California?

<u>Chapter 4</u>

MYSTERY HOUSE

Mt. Whitney, California
June 2
6:30 p.m. (PDT)

With gravity on your side, hiking down should be easier than going up. Nevertheless, it can be painfully difficult since different muscles are on duty. It's like driving with the brakes on and the four novices were feeling it. For Jason, however, all the right muscles were in shape from experience. He bounded over rocks, and around curves, redirecting his momentum with each switchback. As on the way up, he outstepped everyone and had to stop frequently to let them catch up.

Eventually, all the trekkers arrived successfully at the bottom of the trail. Congratulating each other for making it to the top of Mt. Whitney and back, they said their goodbyes and hobbled with stiff muscles to their cars for the long journey home. However, Jason's home was very close, just a five-minute drive in his Jeep. He lived in one of the smaller cabins in the area high above the campground. It was his third year as owner.

As he stepped up into the driver's seat, Jason heard Nate's voice calling him. He turned and saw that Chet was with him since they were driving together.

"Jason, do you think you could show me where the host's RV is? I need to pick up my drone."

"Oh yeah, sure. Follow me, guys," said Jason.

A few minutes later, the two cars rolled up in front of Logan and Sheri Faris's RV. Nate recognized it from the initial aerial view of it when he landed the drone on the roof.

"Hey there, anybody home?" called Jason as he approached the RV.

From around the corner, a large man with rounded features, a full white beard, and friendly eyes walked toward them.

"Ha! Jason, perfect timing," Logan said cheerfully. "Sheri and I made dinner late and we have a lot extra for guests. Who are these guys?"

Jason introduced Chet and Nate.

"So, you are here to get your drone?" asked Logan.

"You know about it?" said Nate.

Logan answered, "Sure, I watched it land on my roof. Somebody's a good pilot."

"Thank you," said Nate.

"It would not have made it back to the summit of Whitney where we were, so Jason thought it would be okay," Chet added.

Nate and Chet were both nineteen, but they each felt as if they were much younger and smaller in this man's compelling presence, talking about retrieving their hi-tech toy. Jason knew from experience that no one could refuse Logan's hospitality, especially after such a long hike. He knew also that Logan and Sheri kept an outside living room they called "the Smoking Porch" where they could talk and eat.

After a nice dinner, friendly conversation, learning about the two young men and their college and career interests, Logan said, "Jason, tell these gentlemen how you got to be a ranger."

"Sure. Well, I used to work in Napa Valley as a salesman for a big vineyard. To find new distributors, they sent me to various places, sometimes out of the country. It was interesting, but I was not sure what I wanted to do long-term. When my parents died a few years ago, I quit the wine business and moved in with my sister, Jeanie, and her husband, Dale. While I was living there, she convinced me to check into working for the Forest Service as a ranger. From the start, this job rang a bell. I caught on right away. I even traded in my 2018 Camry and bought a 2003 Jeep. It had the right tires, a roll bar, and a winch on the front."

"That green one you were just driving, I assume," said Chet, pointing to it.

"Right. It's been a great vehicle for me," said Jason.

"You know," said Logan, "an old Jeep is not really a car. It's a living thing—an American archetype. Like an old friend or a cowboy's trusted horse, it carries its master into the unknown. An experienced Jeep can take a beating without complaint. A brand-new Jeep, though—out of the question. Aside from the price, a new Jeep can't be scratched or roughed up for at least a year or more without remorse."

They all laughed.

"Yeah, that's right," Jason said. "My Jeep is seasoned—scraped, dented, and repaired enough times to have earned its reliable-companion status."

Sheri asked, "What about that cabin of yours?"

"From where I was living in my sister's casita, I would look up at these mountains and think about living here, at least whenever the roads were open for the season. I found the cabin right away. It was just what I had in mind, so I bought it."

Generally, Jason was not one to overshare with those he did not know well, especially about his cabin. But there on the Smoking Porch, in the hospitable warmth of Logan and Sheri and the enthusiasm of the two students, he spoke more freely. He continued, "Before long, I started to notice things that were unusual."

"Unusual?" asked Nate.

"Yes. The first was in the hallway just off the living room is a closet. Within that is another closet, kind of hidden. The larger one has a panel at the back that opens into the smaller one. It was hard to see at first, but there it was. Inside the smaller, hidden space I found a Rossignol parka hanging there, and a pair of leather mountaineering boots on the floor next to it. Obviously, they were left by the person who lived there before.

"Funny thing is, I had just returned my third pair of boots to the outfitter because nothing ever seems to fit both of my feet at the same time. I could tell the guy in the boot department was not happy to see me. However, these leather boots fit perfectly, and they have ever since. The parka fits too. No matter how cold it is outside, these things keep me warm."

"What a pleasant surprise—like a house warming gift," said Sheri.

"Norway," said Logan.

"What?"

"I'm familiar with that brand. Rossignol is Norwegian. Their cold-weather gear is first-rate."

Chet asked, "What else was odd about your place?"

Jason hesitated before he spoke. "Well, this is not general information, but I feel okay about sharing it with you here. Last winter, I wanted to see how long I could stay up here. I had enough food for a long time, a lot of firewood, everything I needed. I was prepared for the worst. I even had a snowmobile I borrowed from my friend Kevin."

"So, it's true! You do stay up here in the winter," said Chet.

Jason continued, "The unusual part is, I did not use any of the firewood. Somehow, the cabin heats itself."

"How?" said Nate.

"At first, I thought it was just a good passive heating and cooling design by whoever built the place, but then something else happened that changed my mind. On a very cold day, I was digging a trench while replacing a pipe. At one point, I bent down to dislodge a rock about the size of a grapefruit. As I took hold of it, I found that it was hot. In fact, it burned my index and middle fingers. That's when I realized there is a lot more to that cabin than passive heating. What, I don't know. But since then my sister and I have been researching the cabin's history and we hope to find out."

Bewildered, the two young men stared first at Jason, then at each other.

Nate said, "How could it possibly do that?"

"I don't know, Nate. It's a real mystery. Anyway, for now, I think we all better take off. You guys have a long drive ahead."

Reluctantly, Chet and Nate complied, thanking their hosts for dinner and Jason for sharing about his life and the unusual place he lived. They got into their car and headed the rest of the way down the mountain. Jason climbed up into his Jeep and started the motor.

Logan and Sheri waved as he drove off. Logan said, "Did you notice that Jason seemed a little nervous tonight?"

"Honey, you don't miss a thing," said Sheri.

<u>Chapter 5</u>

DREAMING ALONE

China Lake, California
June 2
6:30 p.m. (PDT)

In a classroom on level -2B, four student pilots from two Middle Eastern countries were finishing up their debriefing with Alex. Early that morning, they had participated with him in live flight training. Aerial dogfight exercises with Alex were close to the real thing because of the talent and experience he brought. Not only did these four students consider it a privilege to be trained by him, but they knew it would help them live longer.

Among pilots, there is a special camaraderie that they know and experience but often find hard to explain to a non-pilot. This sense of solidarity, plus knowing that their lives could depend on how well they were trained, helped Alex to put his annoyances with Connor aside and settle into teaching the students what he knew best.

Alex glanced at his watch. Almost 1830 hours. Though it was satisfying to know he had helped improve the skills of the four pilots, he was ready to be done with work for the day. A friend Alex knew from his second deployment in Iraq was visiting the facility for a couple of days, and they planned to meet at the only Italian restaurant in town. *It will be nice to get caught up over some lasagna and a couple beers*, he thought.

However, before he made it to his car, an apologetic text message came across his phone from his friend, saying that he would not be able to make it. This was the second time someone had cancelled on him today. At least this time, it was a friend whose sincerity was much easier to believe than General Connor's.

Eating alone was not a problem for Alex, but he did not look forward to the night ahead. Following his assignment to China Lake, he had begun having sleep issues for the first time ever—dreams.

Decent music and Italian food with a cozy ambiance made it easier for him to unwind, even alone. A little before nine, he noticed subtle hints coming from the servers that it was time to close. Alex rose, left a generous tip, and made his way to his car. After stopping to get nothing important at a quick market, he stopped again to fill his gas tank. When he finally arrived at his quarters, he found a service document describing preflight protocols for a new onboard weapon, so he read it. Then he read another six pages in a book he had been carrying with him for months but never finished. After mindlessly scrolling through a few random videos online, he got into bed reluctantly, and fell asleep.

Shortly after one o'clock, though not completely awake, he threw his covers across the room, sprang to his feet on the bed and yelled, "No!"

Had his wife, Casey, really been struck by a stray bullet? Was this a dream or was she really gone?

Fully awake now, his heart was racing to keep up with his breathing. "Damn!" He knew it was both.

Two years earlier, while Alex was in actual combat in another country, Casey was the one to die. She and their unborn child had become collateral victims of a robbery. After a year of cutting back on his duties and giving grief a chance, Alex returned to the high-adrenaline work of flying more frequently, even volunteering for important assignments. As long as he kept active, he was okay. But during his current, apparently pointless assignment, he felt he was going backward.

He paced the floor for a minute or so until the repulsive memories began to subside, and he could breathe again. He retrieved the blankets from the floor and got back into bed. After lying awake for another half-hour or so, he fell asleep.

Hours later, as the darkest shadows in the room were weakened by the light of morning, a second dream remained vivid. He was about five years old. He and his birth father were climbing stairs together—stairs which were cut into a gray-colored rock and which led upward toward a wooden house. Both were laughing and singing a counting song out loud in another language. He knew it was nine steps to the top because the last five numbers in the song were fem, seks, syv, atte, ni: five, six, seven, eight, nine. He knew the language was Norwegian, and he knew it was his birth father. That was it. This dream was a repeat for him, and he understood that it was an out-of-context snippet of real memory. Try as he often did, he could never fill in the gaps.

The details of memory get muddled for the very young and the very old. In between, life stays busy enough for such memories to be easily misplaced. Alex did not remember many of his dreams, but when he did, they tended to be real.

<u>Chapter 6</u>

HOME AT LAST

Mt. Whitney, California
June 2
8:00 p.m. (PDT)

This is not exactly a commute, thought Jason, smiling to himself.

After saying goodbye to Logan, Sheri, Chet, and Nate, Jason drove toward his own home, only a few minutes higher up the mountain. The green Jeep rolled over a patchy narrow asphalt road between campsites with tents, truck campers, and people sitting around portable stoves. Lone Pine Creek was making its continual roar as an impressive amount of water passed under the little bridge that gave passage to the Jeep. About thirty yards later, a gentle left turn led downward for about fifty yards more, then steadily up at a very steep angle, far past the lower cabins, toward home.

Like a brooding bird surveying the canyon, the cabin was perched on a gigantic granite boulder jutting out from the side of a steep hill. In summer, the upper part of the rock all around the building was covered in dry brown pine needles. It resembled a big cupcake with gray paper sides and a toy log house stuck in chocolate frosting, some of it dripping off one edge. The cabin could not be seen from the main road because it was at the end of the road he was on, around a slight curve to the right, and surrounded by trees. Apparently, one smaller tree on the right side of the boulder had begun its early life growing in a horizontal direction in the shade before it found the sky and soared straight up. Growing just outside the elevated picture window, the trunk formed an artistic frame for the northern view.

As the narrow road curved to the right, Jason reached the driveway. It wound its way to the base of the massive boulder, expanding into a small parking area with room for three cars, or four in a squeeze. He stepped down out of the Jeep and walked a few paces over to the great boulder. From there, nine steps—carved directly into the granite—led upward to a formidable-looking oak-plank front door.

On the right doorframe, about eye-level for a tall adult hung a brass bell, narrow at the top and gracefully flared at the bottom. Engraved on the side of the bell was the left-facing profile of a lion, a very thin one. The lion stood upright on its back legs. In its paw, it held an axe. Although it was an unfriendly, ancient-looking image, it seemed to invite or even dare a visitor to pull on its clapper cord. Years of exposure had tarnished the brass to a dark brown color. Jason often pulled the cord just to hear the little bell still sing out cheerfully with its original high-pitched ring. He was about to pull the cord when—

"Jason!" a loud voice screamed practically in his face.

Startled, he jumped back, raising his arms in fight mode, only to realize it was his sister pouncing out from around the corner, doing what they had done so many times to each other since they were children.

"Jeanie, what are you trying to do, kill me?"

"All I said was your name," she laughed. "That's not going to kill you. So, you're finally back. I've been waiting here for you for a long time. I have the information you wanted."

"Great. Come on in."

Inside, they sat together at the kitchen table. Jeanie opened a folder containing handwritten notes and other papers.

"Okay, I looked through real estate records, the history of previous owners, and even learned things about their backgrounds. There were so many rabbit trails, but I learned that this cabin was built over forty years ago. The original owner was Dr. Soren Sundheim from Norway. He was also involved in building it. This guy was a nuclear physicist with a second degree in genetics. Sundheim had been living in Trondheim, Norway with his wife, Grete, and their young son before coming to work for the U.S. military at China Lake, not that far from here."

"It's funny," said Jason. "'China Lake' sounds like fishing and speedboats. Last week, a guy from Oregon pulling a bass boat asked me if the fishing is good there. I had to break it to him that it's a dried-up lakebed near the town of Ridgecrest."

"It's a lot more than that," said Jeanie.

"Oh yeah—very secret. You know Todd, the ranger I partner with most—he says they call it 'Secret City' because it's mostly underground and only a few people know all that goes on there."

Jeanie read from one of her papers, "It's the 'Naval Air Warfare Center Weapons Division Military Testing Ground.' Few people can even say all that so 'China Lake' is good enough for me."

"According to Todd, the area they use for testing is huge—as big as Rhode Island," Jason said.

"Anyway, in those days, this Dr. Sundheim had been working on joint government projects between the U.S. and Norway. At that time, the United States government had been directing a lot of attention toward the 120 miles of shared border between Norway and Russia. Both the U.S. and Sundheim's home countries were looking for solutions to the potential strategic threat in that Arctic region, especially as Russia showed more interest in it as well. Some of the articles I found suggested that Sundheim's work was linked to a complex cave system near the Norway coast. Trondheim was not far from that area. I found a few other references that connected a physicist named 'Sundheim' with submarine operations under the ice cap and a tragic fire aboard a ship."

Jason said, "Sundheim must have had something our government wanted at the time since they brought him all the way from Norway."

"True—and he may have been an asset other people wanted out of the picture," said Jeanie.

"You mean enough to cause a 'tragic fire' on a ship?"

"Maybe. At least, it looks very much like our government was trying to make Sundheim happy by letting him build this cabin here the way he wanted it and paying for it as well. It was probably the closest place they could find that was reminiscent of Norway—a place where the scientist could have a home away from home. Perhaps they wanted to be sure their valuable human asset would stay here for a while. They could have also seen it as a good location for low-profile retreats and planning with his scientific colleagues. Who knows.

"Remember the couple you bought the place from, Isaac and Mira Bittman? Sundheim must have sold it to them at some point. There was a record of the sale of the building a few years later. Isaac and Mira were retired science people too—chemists. This cabin must have been a real draw for scientists. By the end of his career, Bittman had left a trail of over sixty-four patents. His formulas made their way not only to just about every automobile underbody in the country, but some ended up in deep space on vehicles no one will ever see again. When Isaac got sick and was too frail to climb all the steps up to the front door, the couple began looking to sell the place. That's when they found you. I tried to find out where they ended up after that in case we wanted to contact them, but oddly, that was a dead end."

Jason said, "They were both very charming and seemed to be protective about the place. They asked me a lot of questions but didn't say much about themselves. I just figured they were sentimental and trying to find a good new owner. Now I'm not sure what to think of them, or what they might have known. We still don't know what keeps this place warm, though. Let's keep looking."

"I'll do what I can. Dale says he'll help too. He has clearances for more information than I could find."

<u>Chapter 7</u>

DEEP STATE INTEL REPORT

Almaty, Kazakhstan
June 3
10:30 a.m. (ALMT)
14 Hours Ahead of California

On the other side of the world, at the same time Jason Greer and his group were conquering Mt. Whitney, a sealed envelope marked Confidential was laid on the desk of Tamir Abilov.

"Tamir, we received another transmission this morning," said the messenger, smiling. "We are getting very close to fulfilling our vision."

"That's good, Rasul. My worst fear is to die without being a part of the true communist recovery. If our discovery is what we believe it is, we will not have to wait for permission from any so-called 'democratic' leader in Kazakhstan, especially the one we have now. We will act and let them ask their questions later when we are in power."

Abilov was a minor officer in the Ministry of Education and

Science. Officially, he was responsible for the flow of information concerning the latest scientific research to the higher offices and, eventually, how it got out to the public. Over fifty percent of the country's scientific research activities took place in and around the city of Almaty, Abilov's hometown and, previously, the capital of the country. Unofficially, he supervised and reported to his superiors on areas of research not generally revealed to the public. Much of this research was conducted in secret.

In the last five months, Abilov had acquired information of a scientific nature that he dared not disclose even to those above him. The most recent secrets were darker and more nefarious than he had ever thought possible. To share them with the leaders he felt were moving the country in the wrong direction was for him, out of the question.

Abilov continued, "Declaring Kazakhstan as an independent, capitalist country so many years ago was the biggest mistake they could have made. I knew it at the time, as a young man, and only wish I could have stopped it. After more than thirty years of this 'capitalism,' our only progress has been to exchange one corrupt, so-called 'president' for a brand new one. I watched the last one hire, fire, and shuffle people in and out of positions to fit his own agenda rather than what is good for the country. Surely the people will be eager to go back to the old regime."

Rasul added to his rant in agreement, "The proverb says it best. His private motto was, 'Everything for friends, but the law for the people.'"

"It is true, Rasul, and it was also true that he used his power to create a layer of wealthy people. They claim they have brought capitalism, but they rule like dictators. It is no different from a dictatorship. At least they continue to trust me as one of their own. Somehow, I always knew that one day I would play a part in reversing the damage the Westerners have done. If there were a god, he or she would remember to include me in this destiny."

Both men laughed.

Though he had adapted to the changes over the years, Abilov never let go of the hope that communism would ultimately prevail in Kazakhstan and in the world. To him, it had to. It was the only hope. When the Soviet system fell, communism suffered a crippling blow from the West, but Abilov believed it was only temporary. As a true believer in this ideology, he felt that it was wrong for his country to follow a capitalist path. His convictions were reinforced by witnessing firsthand how corruption flourishes whenever capitalism does not rest on an ethical foundation.

Abilov's education was in physics, but his loyalties were to the communist party. With the ideals of communism lodged deeply in his psyche, he could imagine a bright future for Kazakhstan—but only through that political filter. He was entirely unmoved by the tragic and devastating history of communist rule from the days of Stalin forward. For him, the most dreadful events, including genocide, were necessary ills in an evolutionary process toward establishing the best of all governments. Had he been in charge, he would have done it all the same way.

Abilov possessed new information from two different sources. The first was leaked from a clever but disloyal crew member on an American submarine who had been hijacking the communication system to send them messages via ULF, or ultralow frequency. Transmitted through water, earth, and even the ionosphere, these messages came across very slowly. A one-sentence message could take four hours to be conveyed, and even more time to decipher—if they were lucky. Of course, intelligence collection is an ongoing practice for all countries—but the encryption codes were the tough part. Unless, of course, the codes were known by your own spy.

The second source came to them in person; a scientist. Abilov hoped the man shared his vision for the country, but he was not sure.

Through these two new suppliers of intelligence, Abilov, along with four trusted members of his inner circle, had become privy to something that would tip the scales for them to acquire what would certainly be a new global regime.

***

"Some underground spaces in this world have been carved out by human hands through massive effort, while others are provided for free, compliments of Mother Nature," Abilov mused.

Abilov and Rasul Musin were leaning on the orange railing at the edge of a one-hundred-foot drop-off, admiring a spacious cavern below them, just a few feet from Abilov's office door—underground.

"I think you are becoming religious in your old age, Tamir," said Rasul. "First you talk about a hypothetical god or goddess. Now you are saying she has built this cave just for you."

"Perhaps the goddess is me," Abilov said jokingly. "Don't worry, Rasul, I am in no danger of trading what is left of my mind for religion. Physics, even quantum physics, is all there is. But it has a certain beauty."

In the mountains outside the city of Almaty, near a beautiful glacier lake, is an outdated science and space facility that lies dormant. Like a ghost town, it is a frozen relic from when the Soviet space program was competing with the West. An array of large telescope domes and a sizable telemetry antenna are visible on the grounds, making it a place of historical interest and tourism. However, below the surface—in fact, two hundred and fifty feet below ground level—was a place of more intense interest, especially to Abilov and his circle of friends. Inside, it was a beehive of activity.

This gargantuan, natural void beneath the rubble of one of the old United Soviet Socialist Republic's space facilities was ready-made for the type of research Abilov had in mind. Because his area of scientific interest was theoretical physics, and because much of the research had to be conducted in secret, Abilov had convinced his superiors that the underground location was a convenient venue. Meanwhile, his motivation to learn military applications of quantum physics reached far beyond curiosity.

Recently, Abilov's new acquaintance, the scientist, had information of inestimable value to him. As a young student, the man had served as the assistant to physicist, Soren Sundheim and knew more about his work than anyone alive. While his full motive was uncertain, the information he shared with Abilov was of a highly secret nature. They also discussed mutual concerns about Iran as a serious threat on the world stage.

<u>Chapter 8</u>

FIRST BRIEFING: THE GAUNTLET

China Lake, California
June 3
9:00 a.m. (PDT)

Abilov was not the only one interested in Sundheim's work. At 0900 hours on a Monday, there was a gentle knock at Brian Connor's office door.

Connor sat behind his L-shaped, dark mahogany desk. Ever since he was thirteen years old, he'd had an affinity for massive, dark wooden desks with an L- or C-shape. At that age, it was a cute quirk in a boy's personality. But now, at age forty-nine, it was a tell. He liked a big, dark mahogany desk because it looked and felt to him the way power looks and feels. From across the large desktop, he could see when the person on the opposite side was intimidated, and it felt strangely good.

Over his military career thus far, he'd seen a lot of victories, close calls, and had numerous promotions. However, in the last three years, people who thought they knew him best—people like Alex Larson—had noticed changes. Connor had become more distant and private. Word was out that he had gotten a divorce, though he never talked about it with anyone. He had also traveled back and forth a great deal to the Pentagon. Recently, he received a promotion to the rank of brigadier general.

Now, his new office was on the fourth floor—going down, that is. Far below the pavement, the underground headquarters inside "Secret City" were made to appear almost as they would have above ground. There were facade windows, like the one behind the General's chair, with pastel blue curtains, illuminated from outside the glass as if by sunlight. Nothing is better than full-spectrum sunlight, but this was artificial. So was the small tree in a large pot near the end of the conference table. It never drooped, but it never looked quite natural, either.

Aware that it was his administrative assistant who had knocked, Connor said, "Come in."

Leslie Hunt opened the door and said, "Sir, General Bundy, and two other officers are here to see you."

Leslie was all poise, focus, and business as she managed the details of Connor's schedule and communications. Meanwhile, her precisely tailored uniform outlined a remarkably compelling feminine form, matched with a rosy smile and sparkling blue eyes. Often, he had seen her leave a string of distracted military men in her wake as she glided through the halls.

"Thank you. Ask them to come in, please," Connor replied.

"Yes, sir, and here is the file you requested from Intel," she said, putting the file on his desk.

Leslie ushered the three men into the office, then left.

As they stepped in, they greeted Connor with a quick salute and, on his invitation, sat down in the chairs across his mahogany fort.

General Bundy introduced the other two men. "General Connor, this is General Stewart Morrison and Colonel Edward Olsen."

Turning to Colonel Olsen, Connor said, "I understand you have been working at the Directory of Science and Tech?"

Colonel Olsen replied, "Yes, sir—specifically the National Geo-Space Agency in Springfield for six years, then the Measurement and Signature Intel Department until I was asked to bring my research to this project."

General Bundy added, "Ed has the longest involvement in our project. He will be briefing you on the technical details and origins of the operation, as well as concerns we have."

"Please, go ahead, Colonel," said Connor.

Colonel Olsen addressed the group, though the information he conveyed was new only to Connor.

"I will get right to the point. For the last year, we have been working with a very unusual weapon and control system. We now possess a lethal weapon that can selectively destroy a specific biological target at literally any distance, without our having to know its exact location in three-dimensional space. With it, we can eliminate an enemy, like a despot or the leader of a terror group. We can do it at will, undetected. There is no smoking gun because it is not a gun."

Olsen stopped for a moment to let his statement sink in. For Connor, the implications were clear, but he found the proposition a little hard to believe. Indeed, he did need time for it to take hold.

Colonel Olsen continued, "The most basic concepts behind this system were considered as long ago as the early part of the last century. More recently, this information has been unearthed or, you could say, rediscovered. The existence of such a weapon puts us in a situation where we have no choice but to make it our highest priority."

"Unearthed from where Colonel?" Connor asked.

"Recovered from our own archives, which I will explain in more detail later. For a very long time, the most basic elements of it were not taken seriously enough and were tabled. However, because of advancements in applied scalar electrodynamic physics, it was revisited—but still without tangible results. What we have today though, is different. In fact, the strategic application of the basic principle was discovered completely by accident."

Connor commented nervously, "I suspected I was being brought into something unusual, but this is way over the top, Colonel."

"You can imagine the implications, General. It places unprecedented power in the hands of those who have it. Even those in control of a nuclear arsenal could be neutralized."

"Who else knows about this?" Connor asked.

"A few physicists have been involved in the research and understand how it should work. However, for security reasons, only a few of us, mostly in this room, are aware of the most recent development that would make it operational in the way I am explaining to you today. Aside from the three of us, there is a physicist named Gerhard Schuler. If you decide to continue our discussion beyond today's meeting, you will be number five. I can also tell you that there are five power-brokering people in Kazakhstan who have become aware of it, plus another one—a scientist who is a loose cannon. Knowing most their identities and ambitions, we must act fast because there is a problem."

"What problem?" asked Connor.

Olsen replied calmly, "The system does not work."

"Doesn't work? Why not?"

"Because there is a DNA issue, sir. It's locked," said Olsen.

Morrison interjected, "With this amount of information, General, we all agreed that it would be right to offer you an opportunity to opt-out. As you can see, the implications of what we have here go beyond our national security. It's about our global future. You can decide to play a role, or you can step aside with complete honor."

Bundy added, "General Connor, because of the importance of your decision, we will adjourn until tomorrow morning. You can think it over, take time to gather thoughts and questions, and we'll continue then. If you decide to opt-out, as far as all of us here are concerned, this meeting did not happen. If that is the case, you can let us know before our second briefing. Either way, we will all honor your decision."

"Fair enough," said Connor calmly. "Tomorrow morning."

Never had Connor's office seemed so quiet as when the three men closed the door behind them. Somehow the mahogany desk seemed smaller.

What they described carried implications far beyond his career—beyond anybody's career. But he couldn't help but wonder why they had chosen him to be part of this inner circle.

Of course, my answer is 'yes,' Connor thought to himself. Still, a familiar whisper of doubt echoed in his mind: *Could this be a setup of some kind?*

Chapter 9

MAJOR TOM

Pomona, California
June 4
1:30 a.m. (PDT)

As General Connor was learning about a mysterious weapon, another type of science was in focus in the city of Pomona, California. From the side door entrance, the room appeared to be a high-tech lab at a research facility. One wall was covered with shelves, computer monitors, and electronic test equipment on tables. Along the whole length of the other wall was a workbench, a little above waist-high, upon which sat devices that few people would recognize at first glance. Two silver-metal, green-upholstered swivel stools stood in front of the bench.

Looking from the opposite direction, the room's appearance was more like garage, with a big movable door wide enough to accommodate a couple of cars. Because that is what it was—a garage.

Upstairs, in the house attached to the garage, was Chet Brainard's bedroom. Also upstairs was the master bedroom where Chet's parents were sitting on their bed arguing—again.

Linda asked, "How long is Chet going to keep living here at home? And what about Nate? Why is he always here?"

Dan replied, "I think they are gay."

Linda rolled her eyes. "They are not gay. Neither one of them is social enough even to be romantic with anyone. They're geeks."

"I suppose you're right," said Dan. "He does keep that poster in his room—the one with the girl on the beach looking for the top of her swimsuit."

Linda went on, "It just bothers me that they don't do anything but racquetball and hanging out in the garage. How is that productive? That hike they just went on was a rare event for them. Now they're saying they want to go back in the middle of winter."

Dan said, "What do you mean, they don't do anything? They never stop doing things day and night!"

"Doing what?" asked Linda.

"How the hell do I know?" Dan yelled. "I have to pretend I understand what they are talking about. I run a pool cleaning company, damn it!"

"I know you work hard, Dan. It's not that."

"Look, Linda, I want him to move on with his life too, but how are he and his friend or lover or fellow geek or whatever he is, going to ever make enough money to move out and get an apartment?"

"I don't know. What do you think they are building down there?" asked Linda.

"You mean what do they think they are building?" Dan replied.

"It's a science thing," she said.

Exasperated, Dan said, "I'm just afraid it's a science fiction thing. Did you see that big circular piece of metal crap Nate brought in yesterday? What the hell is it? It looks ridiculous."

Linda offered, "They talk like it's some kind of new invention."

"I know," Dan replied. "I looked up what he called it, 'ULF.' It means ultralow frequency. They think they're listening to the earth or something. This is not what we paid the university for. Neither one of them is functioning in reality and I don't know how to break it to them."

Linda responded, "I'd feel a lot better if they both just got a job. They're so close to finishing college. You know, Nancy said she could get them both in at Starbucks."

"Of course! 'Both of them,'" Dan replied sharply. "Nate is always here because you are his other mother."

***

Downstairs, Chet and Nate sat on the workbench stools in front of a four-foot-large circular copper bar with a wire leading to a buffed silver box that looked like a stereo amplifier. In fact, it was a frequency generator, and in conjunction with a few other devices, it was modified to create ultralow frequencies.

Chet said, "You goin' home tonight?"

"No, too much drama there," Nate replied. "I'll just take the cot."

"How about firing this thing up tonight—see if it works?" said Chet.

"We won't know without a receiver, but we could just turn it on and see if it's still transmitting in the morning," suggested Nate.

"Couldn't hurt," said Chet.

A physics class discussion on electromagnetic transmission had given them the idea for this project. They had learned how ultralow electromagnetic energy can be transmitted through earth and water over very long distances, although messages travel slowly. A simple communication, like one sentence, can take hours to transmit. Chet and Nate wanted to see if they could build a transmitter that would send messages through the ionosphere, a layer of electrically charged particles in the upper atmosphere.

Clearly, this was a do-it-yourself venture, motivated by sheer curiosity. To get parts, they used creative financing. Over the past year, Chet's dad had unknowingly supported the project through agreeing to numerous small loans for equipment. Meanwhile, Nate had borrowed money from his older sister, Brenda, who had a job. Brenda held on tight to her money, as if it were a drug. Nevertheless, Nate knew how to pry it from her grip. A few choice compliments and a promise to set her up with Christopher Lewis was her price. Christopher owed Nate a favor, and Brenda was obsessed with him. It was a fair deal.

Chet announced, "1:43 a.m. We are officially ready to turn on this transmitter. It'll be a milestone, even if there is no feedback. What do ya wanna transmit to the world?"

"How about 'Major Tom'?" said Nate.

As a kind of celebration, they turned it on and left it on, playing a very, very slow transmission of "Major Tom" since they were both into eighties music. Then they retired for the night, Chet to his bed upstairs and Nate to the cot in their "tech lab," next to the extra spare tire for Chet's dad's pool service truck.

It did not occur to them that someone out there might be listening.

Chapter 10

SECOND BRIEFING: GAUNTLET ACCEPTED

China Lake, California
June 4
9:00 a.m. (PDT)

Connor was in his office talking with Leslie Hunt, he at his desk and she, sitting in front of it. He had called her in to discuss the meeting which was about to take place.

Connor said, "Leslie, I'm sure you remember the three men that were here yesterday. They will be here again in a few minutes. Dr. Gerhard Schuler was also going to come but can't make it."

"Yes, sir—in fact, I saw the others coming up the hall," said Leslie.

"Okay. I'd like you to stay in the meeting to take notes. However, just so you know, they might object to you being here. If they do, it will not be a reflection on you; but I will have to ask you to leave."

"Anything, in particular, you would like me to watch for?" she asked.

Connor replied, "Just details, times, places, things like that."

Yes, sir. I believe they are all here now. Should I show them in?"

"Please."

Leslie walked out into the lobby. A few moments later, she returned with the three men, and they all sat down.

"Good morning, gentlemen," Connor said. "You have met my administrative assistant, Leslie Hunt. I've asked her to sit in on our meeting to take notes if there are no objections."

"It speaks highly of your assistant for you to want her here, General, but I'm afraid that is not possible in light of our purpose," said General Bundy.

"Of course. Leslie, you can leave us. Thank you," said Connor.

Leslie smiled and rose from her chair gracefully without a hint of embarrassment. "Yes, sir," she said and left the room.

"What was that all about, General?" asked General Bundy.

Connor explained, "Pardon me, gentlemen. As you clarified yesterday, this is a critical operation. Having her here was my own final litmus test before rendering my decision. I just needed to confirm for myself what I suspected about the gravity of the situation and the need to keep it private. So, gentlemen, if you still want me to join you, I'm in."

"Good. The first thing you should know is, not only is this a limited circle, but there are no records," said Bundy.

"Understood. I do have questions, however," said Connor.

"Go ahead," Bundy said.

"Why me?" Connor asked.

Colonel Olsen answered, "Sir, the answer to that will make more sense if I explain the operation in detail first if you can endure a history lesson. Like I said yesterday, the ideas that underlie this project have been around for a while. Now, however, new applications of those ideas have been studied."

Olsen explained that during the mid-nineteenth century,

physicists were talking a great deal about the relationship between electricity and magnetism. A Scottish mathematician named James Maxwell proposed the theoretical possibility of a secondary and simultaneous form of energy involved with electromagnetic fields. However, at that time, it could only be inferred by some of the math, so it could not be measured. In other words, it was surmised by mathematicians as a hypothetical force before they could prove it. They ended up referring to it as a "longitudinal magneto-dielectric wave," or scalar field. What they were really talking about was something in the fourth dimension. It is not limited by three-dimensional space.

Olsen further explained that, since these ideas were abstract and theoretical, it was very hard to find a way to make money or change the world with something that could not be measured. Except for a handful of physicists, the secondary energy idea was either tabled or not explored as much in favor of what is called "transverse" fields. These are the conventional electromagnetic fields we now use everywhere in the industrialized world, like in motors or cell phones.

Olsen continued, "At least publicly, not much serious attention was given to theories about a secondary, scalar form of energy for quite a while—until a few people took them up again. A famous one was Nicola Tesla from Serbia. He claimed that he could use these hypothetical physics concepts to make a weapon of some kind. However, he was considered somewhat bizarre, and allegedly, his files were confiscated when he died. The question of what happened to those files has generated a whole conspiracy theory itself. Every few years it comes up as a popular topic on the Internet, then quiets down again. Tesla worked very hard, though, and it appears that all he got out of it was a car named after him posthumously. However, the car has nothing to do with the fourth dimension.

"Actually, Tesla really was onto something profound and that rumor about the confiscation of his papers was true—those files ended up with us, as classified information. Even though things were gleaned from his records which led to some directed-energy weapon technology, that application was not the same as what we have on the table now."

Olsen further explained that, as long ago as the fifties and sixties, during the space race, the Russians were attempting to implement these theories to develop a medical device small enough to take into space, like an electronic first aid kid of sorts. But it was much more than that. They set up a research division at a university in southwest Russia. Two scientists who studied electronics, Alexander Karasev and Alexander Nichushkin, plus a doctor named Alexander Revenko, led the research.

"The three Alexanders developed a device called a 'SCENAR,' he said. "The letters stand for 'Self-Controlled Energetic Neuro-Adaptive Regulator.' It worked for diagnosing medical issues and for certain types of healing. Considered a significant breakthrough, it was kept secret until the early nineties. In the United States, we were working on a similar device, but from a different angle. All this was the beginning of the development of bio-energy devices intended for healing people. Most importantly, researchers became convinced that bioorganizms are able to operate within this scalar energy field, giving it off and responding to it, even though it is in the fourth dimension."

At this point, Colonel Olsen paused then said, "I understand this may seem like a lot of information, depending on your own background. Any questions so far?"

Connor hesitated, then said, "No, you're fine. I have an engineering background from college, and I did hear about the longitudinal theory, though it was glossed over. That was quite a while ago, but I am following you."

Olsen continued, "Okay, good. So, all this research focused on the effects of both types of electromagnetic energy waves on biological organisms—specifically, individual cells. For one of the projects, an objective was to use scalar carrier waves to deliver healthy DNA information through longitudinal wave energy over a distance to stimulate physical healing for illnesses.

"One of the scientists involved in this was named Soren Sundheim. Although he was from Norway, he worked with us on other projects here at China Lake. Sundheim came up with a way to use DNA to transfer energy as well as genetic information from one place to another using longitudinal waves. Einstein had previously used the term 'spooky' to describe this type of science. The spooky thing about Sundheim's work is that you don't have to know where the bio-target is in space as long as you have a sample of its DNA. It seems to operate apart from the usual limits of three-dimensional space. There are certain characteristics of DNA that facilitate the quantum transfer of energy. Sundheim discovered the potential of this genetic information transfer as a weapon."

Connor said, "A weapon?"

"That's right—and he discovered it completely by accident. Initially, he was working on it as a bio-energy device, and he was delighted when he could demonstrate that it actually worked. Then, one day during an experiment, Sundheim and his assistant suddenly experienced a power spike, and he effectively blew up a rabbit."

"What do you mean, he blew up a rabbit?" asked Connor.

"He was preparing a sample of DNA from a rabbit with genetically predictable cancer. The rabbit was about fifty meters away in another room when the voltage spiked, and the rabbit suddenly turned into mush."

"Oh, jeez," Connor exclaimed.

"Sundheim replicated the spike over and over, which resulted in a lot of dead rodents and rabbits in various chosen locations, even as much as two thousand miles away. In one experiment, he took a sample of a rabbit's DNA in the form of blood, then had his assistant take the rabbit on a trip to a place intentionally unknown by Sundheim. When he turned it on, the rabbit died on the spot."

"This guy was not much of an animal lover," quipped Connor.

"Yeah, but as he realized the implications of his discovery, he was terrified. Whoever has this weapon could bring the world to its knees without even being discovered. Leaders, diplomats, and other people of interest would just die without any recourse or a known cause.

"According to one of the ledgers kept by his assistant, over the next two years, Sundheim devoted himself to figuring out how to disable the weapon—and he did. He found a way to use his own DNA, combined with that of a completely different organism, to lock human DNA out of the scalar, or quantum, access. We still don't know precisely how he did it, but we think he spliced segments of genes from an animal such as a rabbit into strands of his own DNA so it would interfere with the transfer of human DNA information in any scalar energy field, anywhere. There are spaces in a DNA strand that look like they are just empty or extra. We used to call them 'junk' DNA. Now they are thought of as "antigenic coding genes." They are unique to the human body. However, they regulate various gene functions, turning them on or off, using longitudinal, or scalar, energy. Any newly formed tissue in Sundheim's body, after he spliced it in, would contain this hybrid DNA."

Connor commented, "The more these genetics guys discover, the harder it is to think we are all here by accident."

Olsen continued, "Either way, we think this is how Sundheim made it impossible to use this thing on humans, at least for as long as significant amounts of his own DNA exist in space-time because it operates in a fourth-dimensional quantum characteristic. That means anywhere."

"So, you're saying this is why it doesn't work?" Connor asked.

"Right," said Olsen.

"How do you know it would work?"

Olsen replied, "We have enough of his and his assistant's logs that show a wide range of experiments even beyond what I mentioned. Then the records, which were unsigned, suddenly stop. Meanwhile, none of our own attempts at replicating the destructive effects of the process have worked, except for a few cases where it made the animal sleep a lot. There are some cases where there are healing effects, but at a certain power level, it resonates with Sundheim's DNA in scalar space, generates a lot of heat energy in very specific bandwidths on the electromagnetic spectrum, then shuts off. He loaded the fourth dimension with his own hybrid DNA to block its effect on humans. As long as a significant amount of Sundheim's DNA is anywhere in, well, the spatial universe, it will shut down the conveyance of genetic information. So, health machines could, and in some cases do, work to a minimal degree, but not above a certain power setting. He created a failsafe."

"So, this guy was a humanitarian, but on the other hand, he was a pain in the ass," Connor said.

"Basically, yes. While Sundheim worked with the United States, he was developing a method to convey heat in much the same way. We think he did a bait-and-switch with us to hide his bioweapon discoveries by using a similar approach with heat experiments instead. He could change the temperature remotely in places as if he had a thermostat. However, his heat experiments involved the exact same collection of bandwidths that we found, and he never let anybody get all the information about how he was doing it.

"Now, there was a research facility inside a cave system in Norway that used to give off the exact same heat energy signature until recently, when it was destroyed by fire. When it was destroyed, the signature electromagnetic emissions stopped there. However, we have discovered two more sources that emit the same signature. One is located about seventy miles from here. It's a cabin Sundheim built in the Sierras near Mt. Whitney on a big rock outcropping. While he was in the U.S. working with us, he said he wanted a mountain retreat place that would feel more like home for him and his wife. Since he was doing weird cutting-edge physics for us, the Navy was willing to give him whatever he wanted. Well, after a great deal of computation and tracking, we finally identified that cabin as one of two current sources with the same electromagnetic signature—his signature. There is enough of Sundheim's DNA left in that cabin to keep the device locked. We also have intelligence that the place stays warm by itself in the dead of winter."

"What's the other source?" asked Connor.

"He had a son," Olsen replied.

"Let me guess—it's his DNA?"

"Right. it's close enough to his father's DNA and whatever rabbit he used to lock up the whole thing for it to have been his father's if he were still alive."

Connor summarized, "So, this guy Sundheim endangered then saved humanity, then covered the whole thing up under the guise of a different research project. Okay. Now, what do we want to do—take the safety off? Why not leave it alone? He already fixed it."

Olsen responded, "The problem is, there is a leak. We know there are five deep-state people in the country of Kazakhstan who know about this, and they have been trying to unlock it. In fact, they know that Sundheim and his wife died, and they have surmised—accurately—that destroying the DNA is the key.

"Meanwhile, Sundheim's assistant mysteriously disappeared. We believe he is from Kyrgyzstan, and learned English at an international school in London. He is the leak. Whoever unlocks the process will eventually be able to use it as a weapon. All that is needed is a DNA sample from whatever target they choose, like some blood or tissue. Since there are only a few people on both sides who know the details about this and how to use it, these few people are the first and most vital targets—for both sides. The only way to free up the scalar field for using it with human DNA is to find Soren Sundheim's and his son's remaining DNA and destroy it. We are ready to act when that happens, but we don't think the other side is—not quite yet—so we need to move on it right away."

"Did you say Sundheim died?" Connor asked.

"Yes, he died on a ship in the Arctic Ocean when it exploded. Supposedly, it was an accident, but we don't think so. There is no trace of him, literally—his DNA was completely destroyed."

"Who did that, I wonder," said Connor.

"We think it was Sundheim's assistant. He is the only one who could have known about it back then," said Olsen.

"So, who are the other people who know about this now?" Connor asked.

"The main player is named Tamir Abilov. Officially, he is the Minister of Science in Almaty, Kazakhstan. He's the gatekeeper for their most secret scientific research information. However, we know he hates the present government—wants to go back to the old days—but he plays the game to keep his position. In some ways, he is the most powerful man in the country already. With this new information, he could take over a lot more than his own government.

"Abilov has four others working with him, but as of yet, they do not have the whole picture. For instance, we don't think they know who carries the DNA. But Abilov is sure enough about this technology to be taking extraordinary and covert measures to control it. He has been tracking down the DNA using a process of elimination and attempting to destroy it exclusively with heat. We don't believe he has a way to detect the signature yet, so it gives us a limited advantage, at least for now. Apparently, small traces of the DNA are not relevant but larger accumulations are—even, for example, in heavy clothing worn frequently or where there was a lot of sweat. So, he is going after any location where he thinks that may be found."

General Bundy added, "Killing Sundheim and his wife was evidently the first attempt at eradicating this obstacle and possibly unlocking the weapon. Meanwhile, Abilov, though he does not have all the information, has been searching for the DNA. So far, there have been numerous fires that we think are linked to Abilov."

General Morrison said, "We have to act as soon as we can to free up the device, use it on Abilov and his team, then relock it once we take control of it. This is a national and global security issue because we can't allow anyone else to get it, like the Russians for instance. It would not only put them back on the map, but they would be able to dominate the world."

Connor said, "You mean we are supposed to destroy these two DNA sources before Abilov can get to them, then use the weapon to destroy Abilov and his buddies, and after that, lock it back up? If we fail, he destroys the five of us and ends up with unlimited power?"

Olsen replied, "Yes. During that window of time when it is unlocked, we must be in control of it. Again, we don't believe they have the advantage of knowing the electromagnetic signature information we are using. Furthermore, we now have the names of the members of their group, everyone but Sundheim's assistant, and we are close to getting that. Somewhere in that cabin is a deposit of Soren Sundheim's DNA and that must go away too."

Bundy commented, "The fact is, we are the good guys. We are the only ones on this side of the world who know enough about the weapon to activate it, at least for now. Abilov will get control of this weapon if we don't unlock it first. Once he and his inner circle are out of the way, we can lock it again permanently; that is Dr. Schuler's department. We will own the key, which is a hell of a lot better than anyone else having it."

It was unusual for Brian Connor to be at a loss for a cynical comment, but for a few moments, he was. Then he said, "Back to my previous question, 'Why me?'"

General Bundy answered, "Two reasons. First, your history of service, especially under extreme circumstances where you should not have survived. You were a target then and, by knowing what we have discovered, you will be a target again if you are identified—though in a different way. Second, because of your history with Lieutenant Colonel Alex Larson. You have both stepped into assignments that were difficult to stomach. We need to trust him to fly a critical mission without knowing what it is about."

"That'll be tough. He always wants inside information," said Connor.

"He can't know. And it must be him," said Bundy.

"Why?"

"Because his birth name is Sundheim. He is the second signature source," Bundy replied.

Connor was incredulous. He exclaimed, "Alex?! Does he know?"

Bundy replied, "Only that he is adopted, what his original name is, and that his parents died in an accident. He was five when they died. But as far as he is concerned, his adoptive parents are his parents. This guy declined a promotion not long ago because he doesn't want to jeopardize his pilot status. He wants in on whatever is important to the country, and he wants to keep flying. You know him, so you know his loyalty."

"So, he's going to destroy that cabin and whatever is in it, and he is not going to make it back, but he won't know that up front," said Connor.

"That's right."

"So, we are going to screw him over," Connor said.

Bundy replied, "I'm afraid so, and, unfortunately, his reputation too. We're going to have to disavow a rogue pilot who goes psycho and fires on a domestic target. There is no choice."

Morrison said, "You will orchestrate Larson's entire mission, what he understands about it, and the way it gets reported afterward. You will also arrange for the destruction of his aircraft, with him in it, immediately after he fires on his target."

Connor seemed to stare at something across the room that was not there. His sober expression lingered. Finally, he said, "Okay, I can do that, but I want to draw in someone who can help. Jim Barker. He's a Marine who works with Intel and has a degree in engineering. We were in school together and he has a special talent for solving unusual problems. I'll let him know only what he needs to for accomplishing the mission."

Bundy said, "Okay. And look, gentlemen, we all know that this whole thing sucks, but it must be done."

Chapter 11

SUBMARINE WARFARE

Ridgecrest, California
June 4
7:30 p.m. (PDT)

That evening, Leslie Hunt was at the Lazy Jay Bar and Grill, sitting in her favorite booth with the cushy, maroon-colored seats. After a day's work, it was a nice place to unwind, and they closed late depending on the number of customers. Leslie was talking casually with a fellow officer, a sailor named Stephan Benetti.

Earlier that day, she and Benetti had met in the second-level lunchroom in the China Lake facility. Normally, he worked in communications on a U.S. submarine. For the last two days, he had been at the China Lake facility for meetings with technicians who were tweaking the guidance system for the Tomahawk missile. He arrived with a group who were receiving tech support for how to use the system properly before returning to their sub the next day.

Never had Leslie accepted a date invitation from anyone at work.

However, there was something about Stephan. Partly, it was his confident European demeanor and olive skin. But the greater part of her attraction was his apparent disinterest in her, at least initially. She was not used to that. So, when he did look directly at her to speak, it felt to her like a kind of authoritative approval. He had gotten to her. They decided to meet after work at the Lazy Jay for a margarita.

"That's an impressive underground installation you work in," Stephan said. "You can't even tell it's there from the outside."

"People call it 'Secret City.' Everybody knows it's there, and nobody knows it's there. I don't talk much about it, though."

"I get it. We both have what you could call 'under the surface' jobs we can't say much about. What do you do for fun?"

"I run, ride very, very long distances on my road bike, and I play tennis."

"How far do you ride?"

"Around the block once on Tuesday," she said, joking, "and if I recover by Friday, I do it again."

"Ha! You are lying."

"Maybe. What about you?"

"That's classified information."

They laughed.

After a little while, she got up to use the restroom. While she was gone, Stephan took out his wallet and removed a paper resembling a small sugar packet. He tore it open and added a new ingredient to her drink, giving it a quick stir.

From the time Leslie got back to the booth to when she woke up drooling on the table with her cheek pressed into her forearm, all she could remember was that she had laughed uncontrollably and seemed to talk—a lot. Stephan? Gone.

"Oh my God."

She waved to the waiter and asked for the check. It read, "Two margaritas." One for each of them. Not enough to make her pass out on the table.

"That bastard!"

She rushed out of the restaurant and went home, lugging a heavy weight of fear and apprehension. She hated to be out of control, period. But she was also loyal to her country. The thought of not knowing what she had said to this stranger was frightening. She could only hope that Stephan was just a psycho sailor playing a sadistic trick on a woman he had just met and that was all there was to it. Not likely though.

What did I tell him?

Knowing her career would probably be over, she also knew she had to inform the General.

Chapter 12

"YOU'VE GOT MAIL!"

Almaty, Kazakhstan
June 5
10:35 p.m. (ALMT)
14 Hours Ahead of California

News may travel fast, but even at a slow speed, some stolen news can travel a great distance.

"Tamir, I have some intel for you."

Tamir Abilov swiveled in his chair. "What is it?"

"We have received more transmissions from our friend on the American submarine."

The message had come via five separate ULF transmissions over a period of three hours. However, the encryption was theirs, which saved a significant amount of time. Each of the messages consisted of a name, without explanation. Together, they formed a list of names:

1. Brian Connor, General.

2. Edward Olsen, Colonel.
3. Stewart Morrison, General.
4. Johnathan Bundy, General.
5. Gerhard Schuler, Physicist.

Abilov read the names with a glint of satisfaction in his eyes. "Good, we have all five. Iosif, take these names to the cryo-vault and see if you can confirm a blood match. Let me know."

Iosif Volkov, one of Abilov's inner circle, monitored ultralow transmissions regularly from various sources. However, he could not always trace the origin. While they could decode most messages if given enough time, others were too elusive. For example, recently, they had been trying to make sense of a long message in English that they designated, "Major Tom." It had similarities to a song. Eventually, they came to realize that it was, in fact, a song. That transmission seemed to be describing an operation conducted in space. However, because everything was cryptic in this medium, they never discovered its real meaning.

On the other hand, some messages were very easy to decode, like the one today—because the sender was an agent of their own.

Chapter 13

SAFETY MEASURES AND CONSCIENCE—DISABLED

China Lake, California
June 6
1:00 p.m. (PDT)

Major Jim Barker had many talents, combined with a great deal of battlefield experience during his military career. Along with a degree in engineering, he had a special knack for devices—particularly explosive ones. Today, he was in a private meeting with General Brian Connor. Held in strict confidence, the purpose of the meeting was to assign him an important task.

Connor sat behind his desk; Barker faced him from the chair in front.

"Major, thank you for coming at short notice," Connor said.

"My pleasure, sir. What can I do for you?"

Connor leaned forward, resting his elbows on the dark mahogany.

"I have a difficult assignment for you. It involves a technical task, but that's not the difficult part."

"Okay, sir. First, what is the easy part?"

"The easy part is that we want you to figure out how to get a piece of ordinance to explode before it gets launched from the plane it's on. Detonation must be a few seconds after a first missile is fired."

"What plane?" asked Barker.

"An F-16," Connor replied.

"What ordinance?"

"Something incendiary and powerful enough to destroy the plane as well as the pilot."

Barker thought for a moment, then said, "We may be talking about a JASSM."

"A Joint Air-to-Surface Standoff Missile," said Connor.

"Yes sir. It's fuel-fed so it would produce quite a fire. Off the top of my head, we could program the second missile under the wing to initiate a detonation sequence after the first missile starts to fly. It would go off a few seconds later without leaving the plane. I could disable 3-d and IR targeting, as well as the AJGPS, and use a different fuse activator. But I'm wondering, is this a booby-trap for a defecting Iraqi pilot or trainee? And is it worth losing even an older bird over?"

"You'll have to let us worry about that. Major, this is for an extreme cover operation. We are bringing you in on it because of your talent and service record. Because it is classified at the highest level, we think you can be trusted to view it that way. Are we right?"

"Yes, sir. Of course, sir."

Connor went on beyond what he had intended: "I can only tell you that the implications of this project are more far-reaching than I can discuss in detail. It is about a new type of weapon and destroying some DNA associated with it."

"Is that the hard part, sir?"

"No. the hard part is that an operation has to be carried out by one of our people, a man named Sundheim, and he is not coming back," Connor said.

For a moment, Connor had second thoughts about mentioning that name to Barker, but he dismissed them, thinking it would help conceal that the pilot's current name was Larson.

"From what you are saying, I assume this pilot will not know about that part; hence, the booby-trap," Barker surmised.

"Yes. And, Major, I realize this is not exactly the way things should be, to say the least, but the pilot can't know. There are reasons it must be that way."

Barker paused for more than a moment. "I've seen a lot of things that are not the way they should be, sir."

"I know you have, Major."

Barker asked, "Two questions, sir. How long do I have and who will I work with?"

"Our exact timeline is unsettled, but we want this piece to be in place no more than one month from now, assuming it is done right. You report only to me, you speak only to me about it. We will supply the other techs, but all they get to know is that you are making a prototype 'booby-trap' to prepare for a completely hypothetical future application."

Barker was silent and pensive for a few seconds.

"Are you up to this, Major?" asked Connor.

"Yes, sir. I am up to it," Baker replied.

In that moment, outwardly, Jim Barker was lying. He was a soldier taking orders. But behind that facade, in the core of his humanity, he was reeling from the impact of a profound contradiction. It was a familiar feeling for him of being trapped, one which often cried out for numbing.

Connor could sense this in Barker because, not that long ago, he had felt the same agony, heard the same desperate cry from inside. He had learned to bury it, however, until eventually, the voice of his conscience was muffled into silence.

After Barker left, Connor leaned back in his chair behind his fortress desk, legs crossed, thinking. *I don't think the Major will be able to keep this quiet. I'll need to make certain he does.*

Chapter 14

FINDING MAJOR TOM

Pomona, California
June 15
12:00 p.m. (PDT)

Twelve noon in Pomona, California in the middle of June was too hot. Chet and Nate sat on their padded stools in front of the workbench, finishing lunch. Nate had an idea for making it cooler in their "lab" without leaving the garage door all the way open as it currently was.

"We tap into the ductwork where it connects to the house, run our own duct to the lab through that window. When your parents are gone during the day, we block the flow of air to the house and divert it to the lab. When they get home, we switch it. You don't think they would mind, do you?" said Nate.

"Not until they open the front door and get roasted by a blazing-furnace house," said Chet sarcastically.

Beyond the open garage door, the concrete driveway sloped downward to the street. Only Chet and Nate were at the house, so no cars were parked on it—only Nate's motorcycle.

A black SUV with U.S. Office of Naval Intelligence plates rolled up in front of the house, blocking the driveway, and came to a stop. Both front doors of the vehicle opened, and two men got out. They were dressed in black suits minus the jacket due to the heat. Their white shirts were wet under the armpits. Both men wore sunglasses. Looking both ways at opposite times, then crossing the street as one, they appeared to be living mirror images of each other as they came up the driveway and stopped together at the open garage door.

Chet and Nate swiveled slowly in sync on their stools. Their curiosity faded to intimidation as the two parties faced each other.

The man with the most perspiration, the one on the right, spoke first.

"Are either of you 'Major Tom?'"

"No."

"No."

"Know where we can find him?" the same man asked.

"Who are you guys?" asked Chet.

"A better question is, who are you guys?" said the man on the left.

"I'm Chet Brainard and this is Nate Collins."

"I'm John Bruster and this is Bud Myers. We are from Naval Intelligence. Looks like you have a little electronics lab here. What are you making?"

"We're physics students. We have been building a transmitter."

"Let me guess," said Bruster. "Ultralow frequencies transmitting into the ionosphere. Right?"

"How did you know?" Chet replied.

"We know because your project has been interfering with our submarines and a few other things we aren't going to tell you about. The Russians, among others, are getting nervous. They want to know who Major Tom is."

Chet and Nate looked at each other, speechless at first, with huge eyes and open mouths.

Then, Nate said, "Peter Schilling?"

Chet added, "It's just a song. We were using it to test the transmitter, but we haven't been able to finish the receiver yet, so we didn't know if it would work or not."

"It works," said Myers. "Do your parents know what you are doing?"

Chet answered, "I tried explaining it to my dad, but he only pretends he knows what I'm talking about, so we leave it at that."

Bruster further explained the situation to them. "Okay. Listen, guys. You can't operate this. We have the authority and a warrant to confiscate these devices and to arrest you both if we think we need to. It's clear enough what is going on here, though, so we're just going to take the equipment. Believe me, if you guys had not tripped such a high-level concern, you could keep your stuff. Your enthusiasm is great. If your parents have a problem with this and want to pursue it, here is my card. Meanwhile, you need to stop with the ultralow frequency experiments. Okay?"

"Yes, sir."

With mixed feelings, the two young scientists helped the men carry the large circular ULF antenna and the amplifiers to the back of the SUV, open the hatch, and load the equipment inside. Both men wished the boys luck, but also promised to be back if they "had to." Then they drove away.

Chet and Nate were excited, and despondent at the same time.

Their experiment had been a success, and they had not even been aware of it. But now their equipment was gone for good. They both agreed it was better than jail time or Chet's parents being investigated. But they would need a different project to keep them busy.

Chapter 15

A SUMMER TO FORGET

Lone Pine, California
July 12
7:30 p.m. (PDT)

(Independence News, July 3)

Lone Pine Resident Dies in Home Invasion

Major Jim Barker, a decorated Marine, died last night when his home was invaded and robbed. Investigators say a side door to the kitchen had been forced open and at least two of the rooms were ransacked. Major Barker was found dead in his living room with minimal signs of struggle and no discernable injuries. Debra O'Connell from the Inyo County coroner's office said the cause of death was heart failure, possibly from the suddenness of the break-in. Major Barker's blood alcohol level was elevated but not to what is usually considered a lethal level.

It is not clear what may have been taken from the home, aside from possibly a few firearms. Major Barker's death is considered incidental to the robbery. No suspect has yet been identified. Major Barker was a career marine with twenty-three years of service. He is survived by his wife, Katie.

***

Suspicion is not supposed to be one of the stages of grief. But for Katie, the sudden death of her husband less than two weeks after they had separated raised too many questions.

At the time of Jim's death, Katie was settling into a small but comfortable apartment in the town of Independence, about twelve miles north of Lone Pine. The name "Independence" fit her personality and talents, yet autonomy was not her real desire. Circumstances beyond her control had convinced her to leave her short marriage.

With the breakup and now his death, grief was tough and went in cycles. Some days she longed for Jim and for married life. But after each bout of agony, she landed in the same place within herself. She had to admit that what she longed for, she'd never really had with him.

It was more complicated than that, though.

I should walk away now, move away. I'm done, she thought. *But I can't! Too many things do not add up.*

She began to keep notes of her thoughts and questions in a spiral notebook—questions that were mostly unanswered.

Today, as part of her solitary investigation, Katie decided to settle a growing curiosity about some of those questions. She drove to the

69

house she and Jim had been renting just outside of Lone Pine. This was where it all happened—all of it, including the beginning of their marriage venture together, and where, just ten days ago, Jim had died. She drove slowly up the long dirt driveway toward the small farm-style house, built in the fifties. It had a steep-pitched, wood-shingled roof. To accommodate a large wooden-railed front porch, the pitch on the front half was longer than the back. Katie got out of her car and walked around the front of it, crossing the driveway toward the house. An old swinging bench was there on the porch, as it had been before, moving slightly and squeaking with the summer breeze. The air was warm and soothing on her face—familiar.

Katie sensed the nostalgic energy of the place. It was pervasive, almost haunting. In the moment, it felt comfortable, as it had felt before. Then she noticed a fallen wood shingle lying in the driveway in front of her car. Bending over instinctively, she picked it up, just as she would have when she used to clean things up around the house and yard. As she tossed it toward the porch, a sudden sharp pain went up her finger from a large splinter in the wood.

"Ow! Damn it! Damn it!" she said out loud.

Shaken from the subtle yearning for what was now lost to her, Katie suddenly remembered her purpose for being there. With her finger in her mouth, she sucked blood like a vampire, stepped back into the car, pulled out some tissues from the console, and did some first aid on herself. Then she headed back toward the porch.

Each of the four steps to the front porch creaked under her feet in a familiar way. On the wooden doorframe was a torn piece of double-sided adhesive tape where the button for a doorbell had been—one of the wireless plug-in types. She remembered that the owner had that installed just after they had moved in. *Who would steal a doorbell?* she thought.

Katie still had the key, even though it was not her home anymore.

When she moved out, she was not thinking about keys, and just kept it.

As she turned the key, the sound of the sliding bolt in the lock mechanism confirmed to her that the lock had not been changed. She pushed the door open.

Katie stepped across the threshold and saw that the living room was mostly dim. She flipped the light switch near the door. No response. Of course. The electricity was off. It was not a big deal though, because Katie was not here for pleasure, and she knew her way around.

She could see well enough to make her way to the master bedroom and over to the closet, where it was even darker. When they lived there, Jim had taken the liberty to build a hidden compartment behind a facade coat rack just inside the closet entrance. When opened, it presented the handle of a loaded .40-caliber Glock pistol with the safety off. They had called it "the wall safe." She needed to know if that gun was still there.

Using the small light on her cell phone, she located the coat rack facade door inside the closet, pulled it open, and . . . no gun. Katie stood in place for a moment looking at the empty compartment.

Who could have known about this hiding place? she wondered.

Katie had acquired a copy of the investigative report after some red tape issues. There was only one mention of an empty, open gun case, but nothing about finding any firearms or hidden compartments. Neither was there any mention of a computer in the report, a computer she knew Jim had relied on heavily. She searched for that computer throughout the rest of the house but could not find it anywhere. The police would certainly have wanted to look through it. However, these "investigators" had come to their conclusions right away, without looking past the ends of their noses.

"Is this simply an example of small-town incompetence?" she asked herself. "No."

Katie made her way back into the living room. As the sun was setting, the room was even dimmer than before. She dropped into a large, soft brown chair—it had been Jim's favorite. In the twilight, she gazed at a large blank space on the wall across the room. A short time ago, that space contained a rectangular mirror about six feet in length. A special heirloom, it was passed on to Katie by her mother as a wedding gift. Her mother hoped it would find an extended presence with her daughter's new family.

Katie and Jim had their last argument in this room before she finally left. In the twilight, her memory played it all back to her as if it had just happened.

That evening, Jim had been sitting in this same chair, with a dismal expression on his face. Katie could smell alcohol. When she asked him what was wrong, first he said it was nothing, that he was tired from work. When she tried to comfort him and get him to talk, he lashed out in anger, making a lot of crazy-sounding statements she had heard a few times before—he wished he was wrong about some high-level project, that it was worse than the genocide he saw in Iraq, that someone he hated named Connor was planning a strike of some kind. Jim became furious, saying he was supposed to help kill an innocent man and that Connor was the one who should die.

Suddenly, Jim had turned on her, as he had numerous times in the last month, accusing her of being a spy, a mole, of trying to get him to violate his honor by spilling information. With that, he sent his nearly empty bottle of Jack Daniel's whiskey flying across the room into the mirror. Thousands of glass chunks and shards exploded off the wall, crashing and tinkling to the floor. Katie's heart had shattered with it.

Until then, her heart and her mind had been pulling in different directions. In her most reasonable state of mind, she knew it was over shortly after they married when his pattern of drinking and raging began. She had found an attorney. Divorce papers were in her purse, ready to sign—but for her heart. She had been clinging to a fading hope that he was hers. However, in that loud crashing moment, she had realized—not only was he a prisoner of alcohol, but possibly something much bigger.

Katie pulled herself into the present and pushed up out of the chair. Once she was on her feet, she made her way through the front door and locked it behind her.

As she headed back down the long dirt driveway for the last time, Katie thought about the past six months of her life; how she had invested herself in her marriage, then in repairing it, then in finding the resolve to leave. Soon, she came to the country road leading into Lone Pine, a town where the main highway goes through its middle. As she turned left onto that highway toward Independence, she reflected on Jim's death, the weird circumstances surrounding it, and how much she wanted to become normal again. She decided to go back to work, get off social media, and see if she could find some real friends.

"What if I started attending a church?" she said to herself. "I heard that the one down the street from my apartment is particularly friendly. I'll find out."

Chapter 16

COUNTER-ESPIONAGE

China Lake, California
July 16
10:00 a.m. (PDT)

Back at China Lake, Major Allen Jacobs, Chief of Staff, had some important news and a few questions for General Bundy and the others. Bundy, Connor, Morrison, and Colonel Olsen were sitting at the conference table. Jacobs had come to discuss the recent arrest of Stephan Benetti and the information he had obtained from Leslie Hunt at the Lazy Jay.

Bundy nodded to Jacobs, who began, "It appears that our spy, Communications Officer Stephan Benetti, had been using our submarine communications to leak information for about three months before he went after Connor's administrative assistant, Leslie Hunt, last month. By the way, she is in the clear. In fact, she helped us nab him by coming to General Connor right away with the information about his spiking her drink. Her blood test revealed traces of Rohypnol and everything else about her story checks out. Lucky for us, Benetti is enough of an idiot to have given her his real name and the name of the sub.

"We have been monitoring him ever since she made the report, up until the arrest yesterday. As far as we know, the people he was leaking to are not yet aware of his arrest, so we'd like to exploit the situation. We don't know his mode of receiving messages from them yet, but we now know the code he was using to transmit through ULF. He is a gifted computer hack. Too bad he was not really on our side as we thought. We have enough records of messages he sent to give us an idea of who the audience was."

"Who was it?" said Bundy carefully.

Jacobs replied, "The messages appear to be directed to one of the 'stan' countries. We wanted to check with you because Benetti targeted General Connor's admin for information and because of the content of his last transmissions."

"What was the content?" asked Colonel Olsen.

"The last transmissions consisted of five separate, short messages, each with the name of an officer plus one scientist, all currently at this facility. It reads like this."

Jacobs passed them a paper with the same list of five names Abilov had received.

"Any ideas?" asked Jacobs.

Inwardly, Bundy was alarmed when he saw their names on the list because he realized the implications. Thanks to this spy, adversaries on the other side of the world now had their identities. How long before they would have samples of DNA was unknown.

With an air of detachment, Bundy answered, "Right now, only that he was fishing for anything he could find. On the date Benetti was here and then spoke with General Connor's admin, four out of five of those people on this list met together, as we often do, depending on our mutual project involvements. However, I'll take this to Dr. Schuler and see what we can make of it. You're right, if you can learn what Benetti was trying to get, it will be easier to turn around and send them bad intel, but right now, I don't know what that would be."

"Okay, General. Thank you for your time."

"You are welcome, Major."

After Jacobs left, General Bundy turned to the others and said, "So, they have our names now. Just hope they don't have tissue samples. Have you given blood lately?"

"No," said Olsen. Connor and Morrison shook their heads.

"Let Dr. Schuler know about this," Bundy instructed Olsen.

Chapter 17

DIY DETECTIVE

Independence, California
July 20
10:00 a.m. (PDT)

Katie could have been a detective had she not followed a nursing career. Unfortunately, her first practice as a do-it-yourself sleuth came when she decided to get to the bottom of her late husband's death.

On a Tuesday morning in late July, Katie was on the phone, waiting on hold. She held the clipped-out news story of Jim's death in her hand and read it over once more.

"There is so much that does not add up. He wouldn't have just died like that, or even taken his own life," she said softly to herself.

Finally, a voice came back on the line. "I'm sorry, we do not have a coroner named Debra O'Connell. During the dates you mentioned, our own coroner was in San Diego, but I don't find any record of who was filling in for her."

Quietly, Katie mumbled, "A skunk in the wood pile."

"Sorry, ma'am, I didn't quite hear that?"

"Oh, just something my dad used to say. Never mind," she said. "Thank you for your help."

After she slipped the worn article into the back of her spiral notebook, Katie took up her pen, turned to a page near the middle, and made a note. As a nurse, she was used to recording everything: actions taken, times, medication amounts, and even complaints from patients. One detail overlooked could have life or death implications. Here, she wrote, "Called County Coroner's office today. They say there is no record of Debra O'Connell. Impostor? They are idiots? They are lazy and don't keep track?"

Then, frustrated and sarcastic, she spoke aloud to an imaginary investigator. "Excuse me, can you tell me what happened to Major Jim Barker? You know, career Marine, combat veteran, promoted numerous times, recipient of the Medal of Honor?"

Answering as the investigator, she said, "Oh, him. Yes, he died of fright in a domestic home invasion. They say the cause of death was, let's see. Oh, here it is, his heart stopped."

Speaking as herself again, Katie asked, "Do your records show anything else?"

The investigator responded, "No suspects, no prints aside from his. Says here a gun case in the hallway with a fingerprint locking device was open but empty. No other guns and nothing pertinent to the case was found in the house."

"Is there any mention of his wife being a possible suspect? She left him recently," said Katie, speaking of herself in the third person.

"No mention of that. It just says there will be no further investigation," came the reply.

Katie took a deep breath, then let out a sigh.

"Great. Now I'm talking to myself!" she said—to herself.

During her short marriage to Jim, Katie had become proficient at mentally shelving many of the things he said and did when he was inebriated. Since then, memories of statements he had made as well as inconsistencies in his behavior crept back into her memory as fragments, sometimes with vivid harshness. The pages in her notebook were filling up. It was a lot to make sense of alone.

As she closed her notebook and secured it with a rubber band, she thought to herself. *I wish there was somebody I could talk to about this. At least it would be nice to have someone to socialize with. The people at the church I visited last Sunday did live up to their friendly reputation. I seemed to hit it off with that one woman. Jeanie something.*

Katie went to the stove and put the heat under the teapot. In a few minutes, the whistle began to blow. Just then, her phone rang. She took care of the teapot with one hand and answered the phone with the other.

"Hi, Katie. This is Jeanie Ward. We met at church the other day. It seemed like we didn't get a chance to talk much then, so how about getting coffee sometime?"

"Okay, sure," said Katie, surprised. "I'd like that."

The timing of Jeanie's call seemed almost psychic. *I guess coincidences like that do happen,* thought Katie. *Anyway, it will be worth a coffee to get to know her a little. Plus, it will be a whole lot better than talking to myself!*

Chapter 18

WILD CARD

China Lake, California
August 10
2:20 p.m. (PDT)

"We found our wild card."

With an air of triumph, General Johnathan Bundy spread the contents of a manilla envelope on the table. Generals Connor and Morrison and Colonel Olsen were seated across from each other at the large conference table in a room adjacent to Bundy's office. A glass wall separated the two rooms.

"I received this update an hour ago from Intel. It's big. We have confirmed the identity and location of Sundheim's assistant. His name is Kasym Nazarov. After trailing this guy for so long, now we know for certain. He's from Kyrgyzstan, as we thought. At the age of twenty, Nazarov left the country to study physics in Edinburgh and met up with Sundheim while he was working on a project developing a unique medical device. After that, he continued with Sundheim,

80

ostensibly as his protege. He's a clever bastard though because he was simultaneously working with our enemies—either out of loyalty to them, which is unlikely, or to sell what he knows to whoever wants it. Either way, he's a schemer, and patient too."

Olsen asked, "Where is he now?"

Bundy replied, "Almaty, Kazakhstan, weaseling his way into a rapport with Tamir Abilov. He moved in with a woman who is a nurse. Her name is Ayana Omarova. Ayana works for a medical facility there, and she works for us on the side. Sounds like this guy is hard to live with—beats her up sometimes. However, she puts up with it for the right motive. She was kind enough to help us confirm his identity and, recently, she got us a tiny sample of his blood. She must have provoked a fight and scratched him or something to get it. Anyway, now we have his DNA."

"What's our communication channel with her?" Olsen asked.

Morrison replied, "Ayana has a Facebook account, of all things, and leaks coded info to her 'girlfriend,' Inkar, who, in reality, is us. She let us know she found an airline ticket in Nazarov's wallet. The destination is Abu Dhabi International. She says he is planning a short trip to see if he can set up a 'sales meeting with an important person'. That is not good, because this maggot has a product any Middle Eastern power fanatic will be eager to buy. Plus, he knows how to make it work."

"Let's hope it's not with a high level ruler from Iran, across the Persian Gulf.", said Morrison. "We would be their first target too."

Bundy continued, "The good news is that now, we have a positive I.D. on Nazarov, plus a tissue sample; and we have the names of the five people on their side who know about the weapon. Now, to top it off, Ayana says she believes she can get tissue samples from those five sometime soon."

"That's a big promise," said Connor. "How does she intend to do that?"

"She was careful not to say too much," Bundy replied, "only that they all use the same medical clinic. Ayana is a nurse and a phlebotomist. She helps with giving important people their physicals by drawing blood. Presumably, she'll be snagging blood samples of each of them. She says physicals will begin there very soon. Then it's just a matter of transporting it to us, which we have already arranged. It should only take a few days after that. Ayana has no idea what we need the blood for, but she hates the people who run her government so much, she'll do whatever she can to obstruct them.

"More importantly for us, we don't want some radical Arab to be in on Nazarov's secret. Whomever he has in mind will be a problem very soon if we have to wait much longer."

With that, Bundy slid a paper over to Olsen and said, "Here are the names of the five insiders. Nazarov is not one of them, however. If he has any loyalties or an overall plan aside from getting rich, we have not discovered it yet."

On the list were the names Tamir Abilov, Rasul Musin, Angelina Savin, Iosif Volkov, and Salamat Tursyn.

Looking over the papers in front of him, Olsen said, "So, we have their names and they have ours, thanks to their spy, Stephan Benetti."

"And our tissue samples?" said Connor.

"We don't know," Morison replied.

"Either way, it's game on the moment Sundheim's DNA lock is destroyed."

"Exactly," said Morrison. "We must use it on them first; all five of Abilov's group, plus Nazarov, and he goes first. Right now, he is the most dangerous man on this planet."

Colonel Olsen added, "By the way, what is our progress on locking the weapon again so no one else can use it?"

Bundy hesitated as if choosing his words carefully. "That part is nearly operational. Fortunately, the weapon is closer to being in our hands, not theirs. We can take care of locking the weapon once we remove the immediate threat. I'll make sure Dr. Schuler is apprised of this information, and we can be ready to initiate the operation the minute the lock is off."

Chapter 19

BFF

Independence, California
September 24
4:00 p.m. (PDT)

"If it wasn't for us, The Bean Bag would go out of business." Katie was having coffee with Jeanie Ward, who was fast becoming her best friend. Typically, they got together several times a week to chat.

Katie's intuition had been right in more ways than one. She had made a few friends during the summer by attending the church, particularly Jeanie and her husband, Dale. From the start, it had been easy for them to get to know each other. And very soon, it had become apparent that they all knew things in common—unusual things which did not fit normal, everyday life.

Katie learned that Jeanie's brother, Jason, owned a cabin that stayed the same temperature all year long—by itself. Jeanie learned about the odd circumstances surrounding the death of Katie's husband—the guns, the missing computer, and the fact that Katie was never able to locate the coroner in charge of the case. She even mentioned the missing doorbell.

Because of what she had gleaned from Jim during her marriage, Katie had been very careful not to share her ongoing inquiries freely. However, as the weeks went by and summer tilted toward autumn, such a mutual trust grew between Katie and Jeanie, as well as with Dale, that Katie was relieved to have Jeanie join her wholeheartedly in the effort. Dale helped when he could, though he was not always available because of work hours.

Eventually, Katie started revealing the things Jim had said when he was drunk and that, at first, she had thought it came from his being tormented by what he had seen on the battlefield. She shared with Jeanie that she came to realize Jim had been referring to current events at his work. His statements were pieces of a puzzle she had been working on since then. There was a project Jim could not talk about, but which he had talked about—to her. It involved a weapon of some kind that scared him—not for his own life, but, as he said, for the world.

Katie put it this way: "At first, I thought he was just exaggerating, but he was too specific and bothered by it personally. He was angry a lot. He said he was being forced to fulfill his loyalty to his fellow soldiers by violating his loyalty to them. It sounded crazy, like when someone is drinking and just rambling. But it was not meaningless. Sometimes he would refer to 'DNA this and DNA that,' never finishing a sentence. Then there was, 'damn bastard Connor, son of a bitch.' I heard that a lot, and that they were going to 'kill an innocent man' to prevent something terrible. During one of his angry tirades, he yelled, 'Connor should be the one to die instead of Sundheim!' It was disturbing to hear, but I did not know what to make of it, so I just filed it away in my mind."

Jeanie asked, "Sundheim? Are you sure he used that name? My brother and I discovered some things about the man who built his cabin. His name was Sundheim."

Jeanie dug out the notes from her research. Scanning the papers, she said, "The man's name was Soren Sundheim. Sundheim. He was a physicist from Norway. Both he and his wife died years ago at sea. Their cabin was bought by other scientists and who eventually sold it to my brother.

"That sounds like it might be a connection," said Katie. "Another name I often wonder about is Connor. Jim hated him."

The next day, Jeanie called Katie with an update. "I talked with Dale about the name Connor. He did some checking today and here is what he learned. There are three military people named Connor at China Lake. One is Private Robert Connor, who works in aircraft maintenance. Then there is Brian Connor, a general, and the third is Lieutenant Mary Connor, an air traffic controller."

From statements Jim had made about Connor which were propelled by hatred, Katie could only imagine him as a person who was wielding a lot of power. Of the three names, it would have to be someone like General Brian Connor.

Jeanie continued, "Dale told me also that he has heard of using a temporary wireless doorbell to carry a bugging device. He says it's an old method, but it doesn't depend on a computer. If someone were surveilling your home, it would be easy, and they could remove it when they were done."

Katie recoiled in disgust. "How revolting to think someone may have been listening to our conversations! It feels like something I need to wash off."

"Of course," said Jeanie. "But with all that Jim was saying, it may explain why they killed him, and even how they knew about the guns."

Katie could see she had gained a couple of real friends in Jeanie and Dale. More than ever, she was determined to get more answers—and now she had company.

Chapter 20

CAREER OPPORTUNITY

Independence, California
October 25
9:30 a.m. (PDT)

For a passionate journalist, every assignment, as well as every setback, can be seen as a building block toward success. Sally Rogers was both passionate and a journalist. The summer so far had been rather uneventful, however—which, to her, was not good. She was eager to be on the cutting edge of some real news.

At nine-thirty in the morning, Sally was on her phone with William Preston, CEO of the Independence News' parent company in Los Angeles.

"Yes, sir. I'm sure it will be a fascinating assignment up there on the mountain. And perhaps we can also help put a stop to the senseless killing of these beautiful animals." She paused, listening,

then added, "Yes, the rabies problem; we'll get to the bottom of it." Another pause. "No, sir, I'm sure I'll be quite comfortable there in whatever cabin you find for us. Oh, a tent? You mean . . . outside?

No, sir, not at all. I'll be just fine. It will be an adventure. Oh, yes, and for a crew, I was thinking all I need is Brent Matthews. He's quite comfortable in the wilderness. In fact, he has hiked the entire John Muir Trail and I know he is—uh, he will be perfect—for this, I mean." Another pause. "Oh, you need him that same weekend? Of course, I'm sure he'll do a great job covering the senator's speech. You want Reggie Willard to go?" She added, trying to disguise her dismay, "Will that be for all four days? Oh, well, sure, whatever you think, sir. I'll let him know I spoke with you. We'll take care of it. Thank you, sir. Yes, and you too. Have a nice afternoon." She ended the call.

Sally Rogers was gorgeous, and she knew it. She had all the natural curves, charisma, and everything she needed to impress the people she wanted in her life, along with a few she did not want. There had even been a time when she dressed as plain as she could to deflect unwanted guys who were vectoring in on her. She would wear clumpy shoes and baggy pants; she put her hair up and even added a huge pair of wire-rimmed glasses. But she couldn't hide it. The frumpy outfit only made her look like a sexy nerd—like she was rocking a new style.

Since those days, she had become more professional, carefully dressed, and ambitious—especially ambitious. She cared sincerely about the future of the world and believed she could help by being a journalist. At times for Sally, journalism was more of an art than a science. It was about a higher truth that she believed only a few truly understood. And she was very sure she was one of those few. Often, Sally imagined herself in the Oval Office at the White House, telling the American people what was being discussed there. More importantly, in her ideal dream, she was explaining what it all meant. Beyond this, her greatest ambition was for an international assignment as an investigative journalist. For her, the prospect of of uncovering the intrigue between nations and the real motives of political figures was more than compelling.

However, today, she was close to the bottom rung of her career ladder—in a cable news service office in the small town of Independence, California. Her latest assignment: to bring back a story about rabid bears.

After the call ended, Sally walked quietly across her office to the door and closed it. She made her way back to the chair behind her desk, sat down, and laid her forehead on a large calendar mat where her pens, stapler, and nameplate were carefully aligned with each other. Taking a deep breath, with as soft and muffled a scream as she could produce, she lamented, "No! A tent? A tent! In the middle of the wretched forest looking for freaking rabid bears! Somebody, kill me! And camping with Reggie?! He thinks he is a comedian! How am I going to tolerate his asinine comments for four days? This whole assignment will be worse than getting rabies from a filthy bear!"

In those moments, so many conflicting desires were swirling in her mind that it was hard to see this situation as a "building block toward success." Ambition for her career, for Brent Matthews, and even for seeing her ideas played out in the country might put her on an upward path eventually. For now, however, she was headed literally upward, to Mt. Whitney Portal Campground, an elevation of about 9,000 feet.

Chapter 21

DUTY?

China Lake, California
October 26
11:30 a.m. (PDT)

It had been nearly five months since Major Jim Barker was given the task of engineering the malfunctioning missile, and nearly four months since he had died in a suspicious manner.

Today, General Connor was sitting at his desk, mentally formulating how he would greet and deceive an old friend. There was a knock at the door.

"Come in," said Connor.

"Lieutenant Colonel Larson is here, sir," said his admin.

"Ask him to come in please, Leslie."

Connor came around the desk and stepped toward his visitor.

"Alex!" he said in a friendly voice.

Alex responded, "Brian, or do I have to say, 'General Connor'?"

"Whatever you like," Connor replied.

Alex, glancing around the office, observed that there were no other people there except for the two of them. "From the email I got—months ago—I expected a few more people," said Alex.

Connor explained, "My apologies for the confusion, Alex. We were hoping to be ready earlier this year, but it just wasn't feasible to bring you in then. We've been waiting for the right time."`

"Five months?" Alex replied sarcastically. "That's kind of a long wait, Brian, especially in this exciting place."

Connor answered, "I guess so. We haven't really had a chance to talk since you got here. How have you been?"

Alex said, "Fine, I guess. I've done a few lectures, some training for a few new foreign pilots. Other than that, there's not much action. I can't say I know why I've been stuck here in the middle of California, though. There's not even any surfing or beach girls. Just dirt. I don't get it."

Connor laughed. "I may be able to shed some light on that for you. We've had something unusual going on that can't be fully disclosed, so we couldn't fill you in at all until now. In fact, you may not like this, but there is only so much I can tell you about it."

Alex quickly replied, "That part is unusual, Brian. Everything we have ever worked on together has been eyes-open. What's different now?"

"There have been a lot of changes from four years ago, Alex. Since I've been here, I've had a top-down view of our involvement internationally that you and I couldn't get looking out of a fighter canopy."

"Like what, exactly?" Alex asked.

"The problem is, I can't tell you everything—as much as I wish I could," said Connor evasively.

"I heard you and Margie got divorced," said Alex, forcing the topic.

"That's not quite what I meant, but who told you?"

"Eric first, then I called Margie to get it direct," said Alex. "I was sorry to hear it."

"Yeah, so I guess that's one of the changes. But there are bigger concerns."

"All right," said Alex.

"We need you to fly a mission. It will be very brief, simple, and done. Then you are out of here."

"Where?" asked Alex.

"You mean where after that?"

"No, where is the assignment, and what's behind it?"

"It's local, and unfortunately, I can only give you a small amount of information about what's behind it. But, trust me, it is priority."

"What the hell are you talking about?" Alex asked, annoyed.

"Here is the simplest way to say it. Without knowing the whole picture, we need you to fly over to Mt. Whitney, take out a certain cabin in the woods, then fly over to Groom Lake in Nevada and disappear."

With a critical tone, Alex said, "Brian. General. Sir. I think you just said you want me to go and blow up a private, domestic target, possibly where someone is living, and I don't get to know the reason why. Is that right?"

Connor pushed back, "That's right, except we don't need you to just blow it up. We need it to be incinerated. We will make sure nobody is in the structure and we will take care of PR."

Alex snapped, "Isn't there something in the Constitution that says we don't do that? The oath is to uphold the Constitution, not just obey orders. Isn't this against the law?"

Connor was getting angry now. "I thought you might be a stubborn ass about this, Alex. Okay, I can tell you only this. You're right. We don't do this. It is what makes us different from other countries. I know our loyalty is not to a leader. It's to the country and the rulebook that defines it, the Constitution. But we have a big dilemma here. There is something in that little house that poses an existential threat to the United States as a country. If we don't destroy it, the country goes away, and it gets even worse than that."

"What is it, a weapon?" asked Alex.

"Something like that. It involves the DNA of the son of a bitch who built it. That's all I can tell you. That's it."

"Why me?"

Connor's anger was rising. "Damn you, Alex! You won't let up. It's because you are trusted and proven. You are a known quantity. You have faced the worst situations and you can handle a tough dilemma that would disable someone else. It threatens the future of this country as well as the rest of the world, damn it! We need this done."

"Who is 'we'?" Alex insisted.

"Some starred generals and a physicist, that's who!" Connor couldn't hide the bulging veins in his neck and his red face. From that, Alex could tell Connor was telling him the truth—plus more than he had intended to.

"Morrison?" Alex insisted. He carried his own doubts about General Morrison from experience.

"No more, Alex, just trust me for once!"

"Shit," said Alex dismissively.

"Exactly," Connor replied.

Chapter 22

LAST CAMP OF THE SEASON

Mt. Whitney, California
November 2
2:15 p.m. (PDT)

"Shen, what if nobody comes?" Sadie asked.

"Don't worry," he replied, "they will be here. If not, we'll have enough marshmallows for twenty people all to ourselves!"

He looked on with amusement as Sadie and her friend Gina, both sixteen, struggled to carry an orange ten-gallon water jug, the kind with a spigot near the bottom, from the back of Shen's SUV. They each held onto a handle with both hands. At the picnic table, they hefted it up just enough to edge it onto the flat concrete surface.

Even as autumn was fading to winter, Mt. Whitney continued to beckon people to itself. They came for many reasons: fishing, the prospect of much-needed rest, or, like Shen and his group, a last look and smell of pines before the snowy season begins.

Shen Kuan and his wife, Li Jing, had arrived at the camp earlier that day. Originally from Beijing, China, they came to the United

States to escape religious persecution, and, eventually, Shen became pastor of the Protestant church in Independence where Sadie attended. Shen, Li Jing, and the two girls were the first of a larger group to arrive at campsite number thirteen, and they were busy setting things up.

"Hey girls, did you know that some people think you are sisters?" asked Shen.

Sadie replied, "We went to the same middle school and grade school together. Now, we are both sophomores."

"We are kind of alike," said Gina.

"How did you get out of school to come here?"

Sadie said, "Our moms wrote notes to the school. They are friends and help each other out. Too bad they couldn't be here too. We don't have dads."

"My dad went on a fishing trip when I was in fifth grade, but I guess he forgot to come back," joked Gina. Humor was how she got by, and sometimes it was almost convincing.

"Very funny," said Shen.

Since Shen and Li Jing had met both their mothers a few times, he knew Gina's mom, Jessie, was super responsible and committed to Gina; but she was also lonely. She loved her daughter, but between work and single mothering, she was getting tired in every way. More and more, she was becoming less and less able to keep up.

Jessie was glad her daughter had Sadie as a friend, and that she went to that church where the people accepted her. She often thought of going with Gina, but she was afraid she would feel judged. However, the more she heard about the pastor from Gina, the more she wished her daughter could have a father figure. She had confided to Li Jing that, at times, she thought about settling on just about any man to fill that role in Gina's life, but she knew that approach would only be a rerun for her.

Sadie's mother worked part-time at the county attorney's office, where she did secretarial work, and part-time at Ransack's Hardware. Francine was her name, but everyone called her Finnie. As a single mom, she had never officially married.

Shen's thoughts were interrupted when a blue Ford F-150 turned into the site parking space. Larry Gordon got out—a big man with hair on his chin and mustache but none on his head. He called, "Hey, everybody! You made it!"

Shen and the others called back a similar greeting.

"Finally, I was able to make arrangements with my work so I could be here today," said Larry.

Looking into the bed of his truck, Shen said, "Great, Larry! What all do you have here?"

"I brought enough supplies and cooking stuff to take care of about fifteen people for three or four days if everybody else contributed their share and the weather holds."

Larry had packed volleyball stuff and some fishing gear as well. According to the plan, it was going to be a few relaxed, peaceful days.

Larry said, "Hey, Shen, on the way up here I was thinking about when we met. Do you remember?"

"Yes, you were on a domestic violence call. It was before you became a detective," said Shen.

"Right. Those were scary because, usually, I would be walking in on two angry people."

"What happened?" asked Gina.

"I rang the doorbell with my hand on my gun, and then, Shen answered the door! He had gotten there before I did and already helped solve that couple's problem. I didn't have to do anything. We have been friends ever since."

The two friends were ready for a couple of relaxed, peaceful days—at least, that was the plan.

Chapter 23

ON-SITE NEWS TEAM

Mt. Whitney, California
November 2
4:30 p.m. (PDT)

More people were arriving at the campground to join the group from Shen's church. Amorphous tents seemed to bubble up from the ground, writhing and twisting as the owners put them together until each one took on its own shape and color—red, blue, yellow, green. Energy began flowing into the space with people joking and laughing.

Larry Gordon and a friend were stacking wood into a big pile and setting up the firepit for later in the evening. When they noticed it was getting chilly, Larry started the fire.

"Larry, where did you learn how to make a fire?" asked one of the men.

"You don't want to know, but I was a teenager."

Gina and Sadie were wrestling with a couple of tents they had dragged to the edge of the clearing next to a giant pine tree.

Larry said, "Girls, look here. I got you some help with that tent. It looks like you have it inside out."

Gina looked up from trying to fit the wrong flexible tent rods together. A smile flashed across her face when she saw the woman standing next to Larry.

"Mom!"

Gina and Sadie both cheered and hugged Jessie. A moment later, Sadie noticed another woman stepping out of a blue Honda across the parking area. She was wearing jeans, a T-shirt, and an orange baseball cap with her auburn hair tied through the back of it in a ponytail.

"Mom!?" Sadie exclaimed. "I didn't think you could make it!"

"Surprise! I came with Jessie. Where are we sleeping?"

"Over here!"

The two moms and their daughters started hauling sleeping bags, jackets, and the rest of their stuff over to where the tents were lying inside out.

Li Jing saw the surprise reunion and went over to welcome the two women. She let them know, "Dinner is at six."

***

"Dramamine? And you are driving us?! Reggie, how many did you take?!"

"Just four," Reggie replied sleepily.

Reggie Willard and Sally Rogers had almost reached the last terrifying curve in the road up to the Portal Campground. Sheer drop-offs, hundreds—thousands—of feet straight down, lay on the side of each switchback turn. With no guardrail, it was tough to stay focused, especially for someone like Reggie, who had a serious vertigo issue and had taken way too much Dramamine.

One week earlier, a large boulder had fallen from the cliff above and broken on the roadway, leaving large and small pieces on the

99

inside lane not far in front of them. No one from the home office had mentioned that boulders occasionally fall off, unannounced.

"Reggie, stop!" cried Sally. "Look at those rocks in the road! Oh, I wish I could drive a stick! Just go very, very slow here, okay?"

Reggie slowed way down and picked his groggy way tediously around the pieces of broken granite on the road, trying to keep as far away as he could from the edge.

Finally, they pulled into their space at the campground—space eight. For the next hour or so, Sally was working overtime, trying to keep her cool with her partner, campmate, fellow journalist, and work associate. Regaining her composure from the difficulties they'd had on the way up was not easy; as Reggie recovered from the Dramamine, he was not making a lot of sense.

Sally was being as gentle as she could as she directed, or rather over-directed, Reggie in unpacking the car and setting up their camp. Apart from the extenuating circumstances, and the drug in his system, Reggie was quite competent. He might have done it by himself and even had some fun at it. However, Sally boiled over when she made a startling realization.

"One tent!? Reggie, where is the other tent?"

"I don't know. They said everything we needed was right here," said Reggie.

Sally said, "Well, obviously, they left your tent out."

"Oh, not a problem. Look, this says '3-Person Tent.' It has plenty of room for both of us," Reggie said.

"Oh, no. I just can't. No offense toward you, Reggie, but I need to have my own tent."

"Sally, the temperature tonight is going down. It's going to snow. We need to both be inside."

"I know, that's why I thought they would have gotten us a real cabin with separate rooms! But no!"

"It'll be okay, Sally. We can make it a 'two-dog night,'" said Reggie.

"Reggie, I can't believe you said that!"

"It was a joke. Sally, you know I'm gay, right? You have nothing to worry about."

"I know, Reggie, and really, I have complete respect for you. I do. I'm not worried about you. It's just that I don't like to camp, much less *with* someone."

"I think we are stuck, Sally. Here, you can take the cot and I'll sleep on this air mattress on the ground."

Then Sally said, "I'm going to see if the camp host can help."

"Okay, but it will be a lot warmer with us together. We can tell stories," Reggie said.

"Ooooh!" Sally said, exasperated.

She started walking toward the camp host's RV but, realizing it was getting chilly, she turned back and grabbed her down-filled coat. Then, walking up the path alongside the creek, she gradually became aware of the rushing water sound saturating the clean air among the trees. For a few moments, she felt her entire body start to relax as if there was such a thing as "relaxing." Briefly, she stopped in her tracks, then walked on, slower now, and took a full breath.

Her peaceful respite was short-lived because, in a few minutes, she had made it the rest of the way to the RV.

Seeing her approach, Logan said, "Hi, what can I do for you?"

"Hi, I'm Sally Rogers, and I'm a journalist with Independence News, here for a few days."

"Hello, Sally, I'm Logan Faris. My wife, Sheri, and I live right here, at least until the third storm."

"The third storm?" asked Sally.

"Oh, yeah—after the third storm of the season, you can't get in or out of here because of the snow, so the Forest Service closes the roads."

"Well, when will the first storm hit?" she asked.

Logan replied, "We were just talking about that. Could be any time. Maybe even tonight. Maybe not."

Sally, getting to her purpose, explained, "Oh, okay. Well, Logan, my partner or, I mean, fellow journalist, and I are here doing a story on the rabid bears, and I think we are going to need another tent."

"What rabid bears?" asked Logan.

"I'm sure you are aware of the reports of bears here," said Sally.

"Tell you what, Sally, come on over here and make yourself comfortable. We keep this space as a kind of outdoor living room. We like to call it 'the Smoking Porch.' Sheri is not too keen on the 'smoking' part since we are in a national forest but, well, we are careful. You can come anytime we're here and talk about whatever you like." Then, looking at Sheri standing next to a couch, he said, "Sheri, this is Sally. She's here to investigate rabid bears."

"Oh?" said Sheri with a puzzled tone.

Logan asked, "Sally, would you like something to drink? Bailey's Irish Cream, Coke, coffee?"

"No thank you, Logan, perhaps later. No, wait, a little Bailey's would be nice right now, thank you," she said.

"Sure. Now, about those bears. We have a lot of bears. In fact, if you hear an airhorn, that's a general warning that someone has seen one in the camp. They don't usually want you though—they want your food. So, make sure you keep your food separated and not in your car, or they will smell it and pry their way in."

"Into the car? How do you keep them out? Where do you put the food?" Sally took a gulp of whiskey.

"In the metal containers at the campsite. And, Sally, I have to say that I've never heard of any rabid bears. However, years ago, there were some snot bears."

"What is that?" she asked.

"Well, right over there in cabin eleven, some bears broke in, looking for food during the winter, when the owners were not home. It was a mama and two cubs. They pulled off the window shudders, got in, and went through everything. When they got to the spice rack, everything went to hell. They broke open the bottles in the cupboards. Then, they licked up all the spices, and that's when they went snot-crazy. According to the owners, there was an unbelievable quantity of runny-nose bear mucus on everything, everywhere."

At first, Sally was appalled. Then, choking with laughter and her third shot of Bailey's, she burst into hysterics, along with Logan and Sheri.

It was uncanny. She felt welcome with them and stayed for quite a while. They talked journalism, politics, and even history. Especially history. They disagreed on a lot. Politically, Logan saw things from a conservative perspective. People function best, he said, with the most freedom to pursue their dreams—or not. Sally was more on the left side of the fence. She feared that too much freedom would result in oppression and inequality. Some would have less than others.

As the late afternoon faded into twilight, Sally was increasingly astonished about two things. First, how could Logan—a camp host and retired RV salesman—know so much about Marxism, socialism, economics, and literally every topic she had embraced in her studies? Wasn't it too complex? However, the second astonishment was—like Bailey's Irish Cream—hard to swallow, yet strangely and deeply soothing. It was that, even though they disagreed on almost every subject, both Logan and Sheri treated her with respect, they listened to her opinions all the way through, and they seemed to enjoy her company. In a strange way, she felt loved by them.

Sally was not used to this. In fact, people who disagreed with her generally missed the fact that she really cared deep down. She had built her own steel defense against anyone who disagreed with her. In recent years, more and more people had been throwing labels at each other instead of having real conversations. Sally was good at hiding the pain from the labels that hurt most. In truth, though, she was good at provoking some of these epithets and had a lot of labels in her own arsenal. But today—today was different.

Before leaving, she said, "Thank you, it was really nice talking with you." And she really meant it. Then she walked back toward her cozy new residence. Halfway back she realized she had forgotten about the tent. Earlier, she had felt so angry and frustrated at being sent on this assignment, she wanted only to retreat into her own private tent and go to sleep. Somewhat mystified by this, she wondered, *Is it because I just met two people who agree with my opinions? Definitely not that! It just felt so good to have a real conversation instead of a talking points battle. How did they do that?*

When she got back to space eight, she was not sure it was the right one. The orange tent was fully assembled, folding chairs were arranged near a fireplace, and Reggie was lighting a match for the fire.

"Where'd you go?" Reggie asked.

"Oh, just talking with the camp hosts. I guess we will have to make do. Reggie, I do have to admit, you did a great job with the tent—and everything. But where are you going to sleep?"

"What?!" asked Reggie.

"Just kidding. But the cot is mine!" Sally said.

Chapter 24

UNEXPECTED FRIENDSHIP

Mt. Whitney, California
November 2
6:15 p.m. (PDT)

Crawling into the tent, Sally unstuffed her sleeping bag, gathered whatever extra blankets she could find, and arranged the bedding on her cot. She was tired, but somehow much more acclimated to the environment than she thought possible.

Reggie was at the firepit, feeling good about the fire he had started there. While rummaging through their supplies for something to cook, he landed on a container of stew that was already made up and waiting to be heated. Jane, the office manager at the newsroom, was somewhat familiar with camping. She had anticipated some of what they might need and packed whatever she could find for them which, in theory, would be enough for four days.

In the tent, Sally saw that Reggie's bedding beside her cot was not quite done. She blew up the mattress the rest of the way for him and set up his sleeping bag. It was getting dark. She crawled back out of the tent and helped with dinner. At first, they both ate in silence. Neither of them would have gone out of their way for this choice of food, but in the present setting, after such a weird day, it was gourmet.

Then they talked—about their careers, the bears, and how to keep from getting rabies. It is surprising how going through something difficult can bring people together.

"Reggie, if the bears here do have rabies, how come, so far, nobody has ever heard of it?"

"I've never heard of it. I just assumed it was true because our boss at the news service said so."

"Me too," said Sally. "Well then, it must be true. Tomorrow we can interview people around here and see what we can learn. We need to come up with a story one way or another."

"Yeah. Better that than coming up with rabies," quipped Reggie.

In their mutual state of fatigue, that tiny nudge of a joke was all it took for them both to lapse into uncontrolled, hysterical laughter. They laughed, hard—the second time tonight for Sally. They continued to talk in the flickering yellow light of the fire for quite a while—about their hopes for the future and even for the world.

"Reggie, why did you go into journalism?" asked Sally.

Reggie answered, "My brother and I used to pretend we were news anchors with microphones and a video camera. We were about thirteen. We would go out and interview people on the street, asking ridiculous questions and recording it. It was fun."

"Like what questions?" she asked.

"Like one day we ran alongside a jogger, and I asked her, 'Excuse me, ma'am, how do you feel about ravioli?'"

"Oh my God," said Sally, with incredulity. "What did she say?"

"Well, I think we startled her because she yelled, 'Get away from me, idiot!' and some other insults. Then, she ran off at full speed.

Later, I began asking people serious questions, of course, pretending to be a reporter, especially the questions I could never answer for myself. Deep down, I was hoping to find someone who had the same hollow, empty feeling I did and knew what to do about it."

"I have it," replied Sally.

"You?" asked Reggie, surprised.

"Yes, but I'm not sure what to do about it either. For me, I just throw myself into my work. I'm hoping I can help change the world."

"Oh yeah," said Reggie. "For a long time, I was hoping that too, and maybe we can. Now, I just throw myself into whatever looks good at the time."

Sally was surprised to learn that, privately, she and Reggie had this, among other things, in common, though they had a different style of pushing it aside. All of this was more than either of them had shared with anyone.

It was almost nine o'clock. They were about to crawl into the tent early for the night when they heard music—singing—from a nearby campsite.

Reggie said, "Hey, let's go see what's going on over there."

"I think it's a group of church people," replied Sally.

"Come on, I'm curious. We can walk by on the road and scope it out, then come back and crash."

"All right, but just for a few minutes," Sally said.

Reggie and Sally arrived just as the singing was ending. They stood casually on the narrow road adjacent to campsite number thirteen and listened for a few minutes longer.

Around the main firepit, everyone was sitting comfortably in folding chairs and on picnic table benches, faces illuminated against the shadowy forest behind them. Someone asked Shen Kaun to share his story about how he came to the United States from China. Reggie and Sally strained to hear the voices, which were softened by the thick forest and the steady sound of the creek in the distance.

Kuan told a horrific story describing his early life as a young student at the university in Beijing, about his enthusiasm and hopes for improving China through the communist party. He loved his country dearly and hoped to make a significant contribution. Back in 1989, he joined many other students in a peaceful protest of the undemocratic practices of the government at a place called Tiananmen Square. Suddenly, a brutal and deadly crackdown by the government resulted in the killing of student protesters numbering in the thousands. Although Kuan survived, he was identified as a suspect. In the weeks that followed, he came under heavy surveillance and repeated interrogation for speaking out for what he considered to be positive change. He discovered that being patriotic was accepted but speaking out for any type of real change was not. For a leader and extrovert, that was difficult to handle. Meanwhile, his love for learning continued, and during that time, he learned about the core elements of Christianity. Shen explained that when he adopted a personal faith in Christ, it filled a void within himself.

Nevertheless, his new faith led to a lot more trouble from that point forward. Kuan went on to describe being put in jail for five months for sharing what he had learned, as well as being routinely tortured along with many others. When he got out, he was informed by officials that he had lost the right to pursue the profession he had been working toward in school. Expressing his opinions and being enthusiastic about his faith won him the severe title of "political dissident." Not long after that, he married Li Jing. Kuan explained that, when she became pregnant, it was without permission from the government, so she, like countless other Chinese women, would be forced to undergo an abortion. Rather than submitting to that loss, and more severe punishment, they fled to the United States. Later, they had a son and a daughter, both of whom were now adults pursuing careers in Atlanta, Georgia.

"Let's go, Reggie. This is too much for me."

"Too much what?"

"It's just really sad. How can he possibly be okay?"

"It's something about the way he relates to his faith maybe. It's very different."

"I just want to go to bed."

"I know. I'm with you, girl."

"Don't get any ideas, boy."

"No problem here, but if there was, you would be the one."

They laughed.

***

Snow was falling. The down sleeping bag was warmer than Sally expected. Surprisingly, the tent was not that bad inside after a few minutes. They both fell fast asleep without a single toss or turn—until about two a.m. when "RRAAAAAAAAAAAAAA!" A horn was belching out a flood of noise. Someone yelled, "Bear!" from a few spaces away. Sally sprang off her cot and landed on top of Reggie.

"What the—" he yelled.

Initially, she was swamped with confusion and panic, but coming more into consciousness, she remembered Logan telling her she might hear a horn if a bear is snooping for food. A bear had been trying to get into someone's food and they had just used the horn to chase it away.

"Reggie, we have to check the food to make sure it's in the locker!"

"I put it in there. We're good. We can go back to sleep."

"Oh. Okay. Thank you. Wait, you know about bears?" she asked.

"Oh, yeah—they only want your food, not you."

Sally started to climb back onto her cot.

"It's okay, you can stay down here for a while if you want. It will be warmer."

She did stay, in her down sleeping bag lying next to him. They slept, with the bears outside and snow collecting on the fly roof of the tent. The first storm had come, and it wasn't so bad.

About nine o'clock the next morning, they awoke. The sun was high enough for the day to be in process. People in each campsite were arranging their stuff, cooking, and talking loudly. A few were carrying fishing poles toward the welcoming creek.

Embarrassed at their sleeping situation and struggling to get up, Sally said, "Oh. Reggie, I'm so sorry—I just couldn't get back onto my cot. I was so tired."

"That's okay. Nothing to worry about—I mean, I offered, and as far as I'm concerned, it's nobody's business either. You know how things get distorted."

"Oh, yeah. Thank you," she said.

<u>Chapter 25</u>

ALONE LONG ENOUGH

Mt. Whitney, California
November 3
4:30 p.m. (PDT)

Jason Greer enjoyed his little cabin. Like his relatively new career, it resonated with something inside him. Somehow, it was tied to his most ideal self. Along with that came a feeling of hope for the future. Still, he had no idea what kept the place so warm, even during last night's snow.

Officially, the snowfall was considered the first storm of the season. Consequently, he and other rangers would begin watching for people on the trails who got caught out in the severe cold, which is a real danger. Some of those who got into trouble were just naïve. They would come up from the California beaches in shirtsleeves, go on "a little hike," and get a big surprise. Others were more serious hikers who relied too much on the weather forecast and underestimated how suddenly things can change. Either way, Jason was one of the available rescuers.

This afternoon, he was on the couch, his feet on the glass-topped coffee table and a book in his hands. Page one. He read the first paragraph for the third time, not because it was so interesting, but because he couldn't concentrate. Almost as if he had not realized it before, it occurred to him that he was alone. He was sitting on a very big, comfortable couch. Alone.

He thought, *Something is wrong with this picture. This couch was made with more than just me in mind. Plus, this would be such a great place to share with the right woman. Maybe it's time for that.*

His phone rang. Because it was a Forest Service phone, the connection was always made by satellite so, wherever he went, he never had to worry about interference caused by terrain.

A male voice on the phone said, "Jason, Todd."

"Hey, Todd."

"Just letting you know that the boss wants you to check out the trail to Meysan Lake since you live so close to it. He says there were two separate parties headed in that direction. One had climbers—two of them. He wants to check on their status since it snowed last night."

"You bet. I'll go up there and keep you apprised, then be back home this evening," said Jason.

"Thanks, bud."

***

Sally and Reggie decided to visit the little store at the upper end of the road, where the trailhead was. Maybe someone there would know about the bear situation. A guy named Greg was the manager and had been for many years.

"Rabid bears? Ahh, ha, ha, ha," was Greg's initial response to their question.

Greg was in a good mood that day and thought they were playing with him. Slowly, however, it dawned on him that they were serious.

Backtracking, Greg said, "Well, there might be a rabid bear somewhere, but God, I hope not. What should I look for? Does it foam at the mouth or attack people or what?"

"We don't really know, Greg. Sally and I are investigating it to write a story."

"Who told you they were here?"

"Our boss," said Sally.

"Well, sorry I can't help with that. Have you tried the Forest Service? There's a ranger named Jason Greer who lives up here. I saw him earlier and he was headed home. He has a cabin, number thirty-one. It's past the campsites and all the way up the hill. It's the highest one up there and it sits on a big rock."

Sally was becoming anxious. She didn't want anything to do with rabid bears or even normal bears, but she needed to get a story to Mr. Preston.

"Okay, thank you, Greg."

From the store, they drove back down through the campground, past their own tent space, across the creek bridge, and started up a very steep hill toward cabin number thirty-one, the highest. Jason's Jeep was parked alongside the boulder on which the cabin rested. Pulling in behind it, they got out and ascended the granite steps to the landing at the front entrance. Reggie pulled twice on the cord dangling from the bell at the front door.

Jason opened the door. "Hello."

"Hi, my name is Sally Rogers, and this is Reggie Willard. Greg at the store said you might be able to help us with something."

"Sure, come on in."

They stepped into the living room.

"Oh, it's so nice and warm in here," said Sally.

"Have a seat," Jason said, gesturing toward the couch.

Sally looked it over with obvious interest and sat down, as did Reggie. "This sure is a big couch, and so comfy."

"Just a little while ago, I was thinking it would be nice to share it with someone—I mean, with people. What can I do for you?" said Jason.

They explained the story they were here to cover. As Jason listened, his expression was perplexed and entranced at the same time. He was somewhat perplexed by the bear problem and, without a doubt, entranced by Sally. Momentarily, he broke himself out of it and focused on the question.

"I have to say, I've never run into a bear in that condition, at least not that I know of. Does it foam at the mouth, or what?" Jason replied.

"We were hoping you could tell us that," Sally said.

"Maybe it will help just to know that I've never heard of it. I could ask around tomorrow with some of the other Forest Service people. How would I get a hold of you?"

This was a smart move on Jason's part—a great way to get her number. However, Reggie gave him his card instead.

As they were starting to leave, Sally wandered across the room and gazed out the picture window at the canyon below, then up at the sky.

"Thank you so much for talking with us, Jason. By the way, it's such a beautiful view! Oh, it looks like a new batch of snow clouds are coming in."

Jason responded, "Right. There is supposed to be more snow later tonight than there was last night. Well, come back any time."

"Okay, thank you. Bye."

As Reggie and Sally stepped back outside, they felt the bite of cold air as they made their way back down the steps to the car. Both felt somewhat discouraged, especially Sally. She climbed in, slumped in her seat, and sighed. "Why does nobody seem to know anything about this story but Mr. Preston? He was so sure. Then I was so sure."

They drove down the steep incline again to the campground. After a few more fruitless interviews with hikers, a road construction crew, and a guy named Tom, who was fishing, they started heading back to their campsite. From the bridge, Reggie spotted the pastor—the one who had been telling his life story the night before. Reggie turned aside to see about doing one last interview. Sally told him she was interviewed out and that he could do it, but she was headed back to their tent.

Reggie found Shen Kuan near the firepit and greeted him. He explained the assignment and that he was here with a fellow reporter.

"I wish I could help, but I have never heard of this problem," said Shen. Turning to Larry, Shen said, "Larry, have you ever encountered a rabid bear all the time you have been with the Highway Patrol?"

Larry thought about it and said, "Nope, but I did run into a rabid possum once. Just about got bit. It wasn't up here, though. A kid had it in Lone Pine as a pet for a while. That thing was foaming at the mouth. No bears, though."

Shen said, "Reggie, come back in one hour. We will have dinner ready. You are welcome to join us. Bring the young lady who is with you."

Reggie had already considered the other options they had for dinner, all contained in the cardboard box Jane had packed for them. Any of their alternatives would have meant labor he did not want, and none were appetizing.

"Yeah, Okay. Thank you, we'll be here."

At the campsite, Reggie briefed Sally about the possum and let her know about dinner plans.

"You committed us without asking me first?" said Sally. "What if I don't want to go?"

"You don't have to go, but I'm going. I want you to come with me, though. It will be interesting, even if it is a little weird," said Reggie.

Sally finally gave in. "Okay, but why are we doing this? It feels a little creepy. I'm out of my element there."

"Free food. No cooking. The people seem nice enough," said Reggie.

"All right, I guess they are just people—people who sing in the forest, late at night, when it is snowing. That's normal, right?" she said.

Chapter 26

SECRET HIDEAWAY

Mt. Whitney, California
November 3
3:30 p.m. (PDT)

Access to the Meysan Trail was only a few minutes' walk from where Jason lived. Then, about six miles down the trail, over the ridge, and into the next canyon, was the lake, which was about 11,500 feet above sea level. Though it was a few thousand feet higher than his cabin, Jason knew it would be an enjoyable hike, especially when the sun began to set a little later. A full moon was already rising.

Snow from the night before covered the trail and everything else. Tracks in the snow left by hikers could be clearly seen. All the footprints he found pointed toward the lake, so Jason kept going. In about twenty minutes, he met a man and a woman, twenty years old or so, coming down the trail toward him. They were moving at a good pace, faces slightly pink and numb from the cold air.

Jason said cheerfully, "Good thing you are headed down. It looks like snow again tonight."

"Oh, yeah! We'll have a cozy fire waiting for us."

"You're about thirty-five minutes from civilization," said Jason. "Did you run into anyone else up there?"

The girl said, "Yes, we saw two guys packing up their climbing equipment at the bottom of the cliffs on the far side of the lake. One of them was hopping around, like he may have hurt his foot."

Jason gathered a few more details and thanked them as they parted ways. He continued up the trail to find the two climbers. Jason carried a small pack with a headlamp, first aid kit, water, granola bars, and a fresh box of Pop-Tarts.

As he drew closer to the lake, he spotted the two climbers coming toward him on the trail. One was hobbling with the other holding him up so he could walk, or rather, hop on one foot.

From a distance, Jason called out, "Hey guys, what happened?"

As they all came closer to each other, he recognized a couple of familiar faces.

"Chet? Nate?" he said.

"Jason?" said Nate.

"I told you we would run into Jason," said Chet to his friend. Turning to Jason, he added, "You remember us from earlier this summer?"

"Of course. Who could forget the guys with the drone? How have you been?"

Nate replied, "Well, we were doing science experiments until some government guys confiscated our equipment, so, as you can see, we took up climbing."

"Yeah, but as you can also see, we aren't very good at it yet," said Chet, with a sheepish smile.

"I don't know about your experiments, but climbing in winter is a little overboard."

"After talking with you, we wanted to see this place in the winter."

"Oh, okay then. What happened on that rock?"

"We had a good climb and were nearly all the way down when Nate's hand slipped on a wet ledge."

Nate agreed, "Yeah, I dropped about eight feet before the rope caught me, but my foot hit another ledge at the exact same time and twisted. It's not as bad as it could have been but my ankle hurts."

Jason examined the injury and took a few minutes to re-wrap it with his own bandage.

"Easy to see why you can't use it, as swollen as it is. You made it this far though, and you are doing it right. If you think you can keep going like this, I'll call for another ranger to come up the trail and meet you to give you a hand with the last part of the trail. You can't stay up here much longer, though, because it's supposed to snow again later tonight."

"We can make it, thanks," said Chet.

Jason called Todd and arranged for him to intercept the two climbers on their way down.

"Okay, you've got it," said Jason. "A ranger named Todd will meet you on the trail soon. "By the way, when you see him, tell him I decided to go up a little further to check out the lake before I head back home. Tomorrow, let me know how your foot is. If you are still in the canyon, and not the hospital, maybe we can meet at the store for lunch or something."

"Great. Actually, we were hoping to see that unusual cabin of yours," ventured Chet.

"Let me think about that a little. Right now, though, you guys had better get back and put that foot up with ice on it."

"Okay, thanks for your help," said Nate.

"You're welcome."

The lake was less than a mile further. It didn't take long to reach. Jason enjoyed being in this environment so much, he didn't want to leave right away. In the available light, he noticed that, about twenty feet from shore, there were six very big Canadian geese floating on the water. The head and neck feathers were pitch black and matched the color of their beaks all the way down to the birds' light brown bodies. Under the beak, in stark contrast, were white feathers that took the shape of a bib.

Jason walked slowly and quietly over to a large rock and sat down to watch the geese paddling around each other, pecking at the water. A few minutes later, the darkest and largest one spotted him. In the twilight, the big gander opened and flapped its wings and paddled its feet, faster and faster, until it was literally running on the water with the help of its overspreading wings. Then it lifted into the air. It pulled up its landing gear feet and glided toward the other side of the lake. The other five birds followed suit and together, they landed on the water about fifty yards further away. Any time now, they would migrate south, looking for a warmer place. Maybe tonight. *That was probably a practice takeoff,* thought Jason.

Though he was sure there were no more people in the area, he stayed longer than he had planned. Jason did not always follow the advice he gave to other people. However, he had an ace up his sleeve. About a mile from the lake, there was a small hidden shelter with a propane stove, first aid supplies, bedding, and some food. Built by the Forest Service for emergencies, it was almost a secret among his fellow rangers. Since it was closer than his own place, it would be easier to stay there for the night, so he started walking. As the temperature dropped, his parka and boots—the ones he had discovered in the wall closet of his cabin—fended off the cold nicely.

Chapter 27

GAME ON!

China Lake, California
November 3
6:00 p.m. (PDT)

General Brian Connor was the first to respond to a text message from General Bundy to him and the other officers: "Request your presence in my office immediately. Highest priority."

As he walked swiftly down the hallway, past the closed doors of other staff and officers who had left for the day, he noticed that even Bundy's admin had gone home. Like their five rogue counterparts on the other side of the world, the five on this side spend most of their waking hours these days at work. Their sleeping hours, they spent partially awake from sheer anxiety—except for Connor. He always slept well.

Connor came to the door, knocked lightly, then entered when acknowledged.

"It's time," said General Bundy solemnly. "We received a

gift from Ayana—five blood samples. Schuler has them now. He believes Abilov is getting close enough to take his own action and is monitoring us carefully. What is Larson's disposition?"

Connor hesitated, then said, "Situationally, he is on standby, ready for our order. Personally, his disposition is not exactly positive."

"What do you mean by that?" asked Bundy sternly.

"Because of the nature of the mission, I was, of course, not able to tell him all he is accustomed to knowing, so he is rather angry—mostly with me. Adding to that, the most obvious part of the mission, the part he does understand, troubles him."

"Of course it does. He is attacking a domestic target. Doesn't it trouble you?" said Bundy.

"No. I see that it has to be done," said Connor coldly.

"So, will he carry out the mission or not, damn it?" asked Bundy.

"Yes."

"You sound damned sure about that. What if he doesn't?"

"I put a contingency plan in place in case a pilot should snap and fly off in an F-16 fighter with live ordinance. Two F-35s are standing by, if needed."

"Why two?" asked Bundy.

I've flown with him long enough to know that one might not be enough."

"All right, do whatever you need to."

There came a knock on the door and the arrival of Olsen and Morrison.

"Gentlemen," said Bundy, "Schuler is in possession of the tissue samples we have been waiting for. It's time."

A look of sober realization came upon both men.

"She did it," said Morrison.

"That's right," Bundy replied. Then, turning to Connor, he said, "Notify Colonel Larson to be ready to go by 2100 hours and let me know if there is any problem. Gentlemen, we have prepared for this moment. Are there any questions?"

After a silent pause, he said, "All right. It's game on."

Chapter 28

THE GOD OPTION

Mt. Whitney, California
November 3
6:10 p.m. (PDT)

A little after six o'clock, the food was ready. Almost too many pots and pans were jammed onto the small grill, but there was enough food for nineteen people—adults and kids. Gina, Sadie, and their mothers were there. As if by magnetic force, kids from another campsite discovered the kids from the church group shortly after their arrival. Li Jing invited them and their parents to dinner too.

Just when Larry Gordon called out, "Come and get it!" Reggie and Sally arrived at the campsite and walked over toward him. Both had agreed to stay somewhat incognito so they could observe and listen more than talk. Maybe they could pick up some information about the local bears.

Li Jing noticed them, and because Shen had told her they might be coming, she came over and said, "Just in time!" She introduced herself and directed them to a table with a surprising number of food choices laid out. They were famished and grateful for the invitation. With plates full of food, the two sat down across from each other near the end of one of the tables. Then, Sally looked up and noticed Logan and Sheri coming toward them.

Seeing her, Logan said, "Sally! How's it going? This must be your friend Reggie. Did you find those bears you were looking for?"

"Not really," said Sally.

"Well, that's good! Maybe it's a false alarm," said Logan. "Mind if we join you?"

"Please," said Sally.

Sally was curious. "Logan, do you know all these people?"

"Some of 'em, yeah. They come here once a month or so during the warm season, and once, Sheri and I visited their church in Independence."

The food turned out to be a supremely better option than what Reggie and Sally had found in the supply box back at their own campsite. Logan and Sheri's arrival quelled all apprehension about what to make of the group. The couple exuded a contagious feeling of enjoyment of people that made the two visitors want to stay longer. The other people in the camp were welcoming too—more friendly and natural than Sally had guessed they would be. Shen and Li Jing Kuan and Larry Gordon also settled in with them at the table.

During the meal, topics of conversation bounced around the group like a loose golf ball: what people did earlier in the summer, the best movies, and the best and worst of the internet. Reggie asked if anyone had heard of any rabid bears in the area. This led to stories about weird experiences with other animals. No rabid ones though.

As everyone sat gazing into the entrancing fire, the mood around the table became more serious and reflective.

Larry said, "It's so peaceful and pleasant here, even though it is getting cold. I keep thinking about how different it is down the hill. I know I may be biased because of my job with law enforcement, but there are so many stressful things happening all over. For sure, that is nothing new, but things seem to be a lot worse than when I was part of the problem as a teenager. We can't keep up with the crime. People are becoming more afraid, and way more defensive."

Logan said, "I think about that a lot. People angry, families breaking up, drugs—what do you all think, is it getting worse?"

Reggie asked, "Do you mean with people in local, everyday life, or world events?"

"Oh, I mean both," said Logan. "I keep up with news from many different sources because I always suspect there is a whole lot more going on behind the scenes than we are being told. Sheri tells me I should cut back on it. But street crime, high-level crime, people arguing instead of discussing, leaders going back on their promises—either the newspeople are exaggerating, or there is a lot more trouble than there used to be—on every level."

Sally commented, "I'm in the news business, along with Reggie, and I can see there is more conflict—but I'm optimistic. As far as government goes, for instance, I think if we can start leaving the old system behind and evolve one that will meet the needs of everyone equally, things will improve. It will take sacrifice on the part of each person, though. We'll just have to give up a lot of what we want for the sake of the common good."

Sally turned to Shen. "I understand you and Li Jing were involved politically in China."

Shen said, "Yes, we devoted ourselves to improving China through political activities. However, we encountered things that made us think differently about it."

"What things?" asked Reggie.

"We discovered firsthand that those in power were not really serving the people as they claimed. Instead, they were working to acquire unlimited power and control. We came to realize that many of our leaders there, and around the world, are willing to say or do anything to get that control."

Larry said, "In this country, we tend to argue things out, which I think is good. But lately, it has boiled down to only two ways to see things. With most of the big issues, one side of the argument is for more government control, and the other is for less. Instead of thinking it through, people are just taking sides."

Li Jing said, "Shen and I have found freedom here and we are very grateful. However, we are more invested in what we think of as 'the third option'."

"A third option?" asked Sally.

"We believe that there are always important things going on, as Larry says, 'behind the scenes' in governments, but also in the spiritual world. We think God has been working slowly over history on a plan to restore the world to the way it was intended to be."

Reggie joked, "The key word is 'slowly.' Problems have been pretty much the same for ages, you know. Maybe the plan is not working."

Everyone laughed.

Sally asked, "Seriously, Li Jing, what do you think this plan is?"

"The first part is to gather people who are willing to be in a devoted relationship with God instead of trying to make it on their own. Shen and I are convinced that each person needs to have this relationship with God before the time runs out."

"There is a time limit?" asked Sally.

"Yes," said Li Jing. "Along with the obvious fact that we each have only a certain number of days to live, we learned that there will be a day when God will intervene suddenly and rule the entire earth. He will overpower all other governments. It will be a day of judgment."

"It sounds harsh," said Finnie, Sadie's mom, who had joined the group.

Logan said, "Very true, but a lot of the things going on in the world where God is left out are harsh in the worse way."

Shen added, "We are convinced that God's deepest desire is not harshness but goodwill, and we want to be involved in whatever is going on spiritually behind the scenes."

Reggie said, "So, the spiritual part is the third option?"

"Yes," said Li Jing.

"Hold on, is there a fourth option?" joked Reggie.

Everyone laughed—and shivered from a growing chill in the air.

Sally said, "I appreciate your perspective, Li Jing, but it sounds a little idealistic for me. So, you are saying this is all in the Bible?"

"Yes, it's all right there."

About that time, Logan stood up and turned to address the larger group, mostly gathered around the fire. "I hate to break this up everybody, but I need to tell you what I heard from the Forest Service. The snow we got last night was what they call 'the first storm.' Every year, after the third storm, they close the roads because this place gets full of snow. So, I'm letting you know that tonight might be storm number two. It is getting cold. I suggest we all pack it in for the night. See you in the morning."

People milled around the camp, making their way to their tents. Some of them said good night to the two guests from up the road.

"Good night, thank you for dinner," said Reggie.

"You are very welcome. Good night," Li Jing said.

When they had gone a little way down the road from the campsite, Sally said to Reggie, "Now I am really creeped out."

"I'm actually intrigued," said Reggie.

"Yes, that too."

They walked up the narrow road, across the small bridge over the creek to their tent, with her cot and his blow-up mattress waiting for them. Inside their down sleeping bags, the temperature gradually rose, and sleep settled in quickly.

Chapter 29

COMMITTED

China Lake, California
November 3
11:55 p.m. (PDT)

"China Lake information Charlie, one three zero zero zulu; wind, one five zero at eight; measured ceiling, three thousand overcast; visibility, three nautical miles, smoke; temperature, three four; dewpoint, three; altimeter, two niner niner zero; expect ILS approach landing Runway fourteen; advise you have information Charlie."

The Automatic Terminal Information System (ATIS) recording repeated itself. Lieutenant Colonel Alex Larson switched off the recording. He had used up an extra five or so minutes—and that much fuel in the F-16 Fighting Falcon—brooding over what he was about to do. A major reason he was so good at his job—and was still alive—was his custom of gathering information about the objective so he could focus his talents. In the past, if he could not get all the details of a mission, at least he could trust that he was defending a free country against a clear enemy. He had always known who the enemy was. But who was the enemy now? He hated how Connor had influenced him, saying this mission was consistent with his true loyalty; yet Alex did not trust his former friend. Never would he have cooperated had he not seen how rattled Connor got when he was pressed. From the years they had known each other, he was familiar with Connor's quick temper, but this had been much more—as if he were desperate. For Alex, the tipping point had been when Connor revealed way more than he had intended. It was clear that Connor believed there was a real threat, one that superseded the law. What if it was true—that they were dealing with a quantum-style weapon of mass destruction?

But what if it wasn't?

"Shit," he said.

Then, speaking to ground control, he said, "China Lake ground, Savage One, a single F-16 at Romeo fourteen with information Charlie, request taxi for southeast departure."

The air traffic controller responded, "Savage One, taxi to southeast run-up via Alpha. Advise run-up complete."

Alex replied, "Taxi southwest run-up via Alpha. Will advise when complete. Savage One."

After aligning the plane to the edge of the runway, Alex addressed the tower: "China Lake Tower, Savage One, run-up complete. Holding short of Romeo fourteen left. Ready for departure."

The tower controller responded, "Savage One, you are cleared for departure."

Alex moved the throttle gently forward from the combat aircraft loading area where the two JASSM missiles had been secured under the wings. The plane taxied up to runway fourteen and turned left, heading southeast. He pushed the throttle forward again, this time all the way. Then came the familiar roar of the afterburners, needed for moving the heavy load he was carrying into the sky, and a kick from the engine's solid release of power. As he was pushed back into his seat, he watched the speed indicator rise to 170 knots—about 195 miles per hour—the vibrations from the runway escalating with it. As the Falcon's talons let go of the runway, the noise subsided, as if someone had turned a volume knob down from ten to two. The plane made a climbing right turn up to 15,000 feet before joining the route described in his flight plan.

Officially, the plan was for Alex to fly directly to Edwards Air Force Base near the Mojave Desert in California and deliver two JASSM missiles, intact. However, their covert flight plan was for him to fire one of the two missiles while in flight, at a target in the mountains nearby. After that, he would fly the plane, with the second missile, to Groom Lake in Nevada, another highly secured facility.

Groom Lake is perhaps even more guarded from the public eye than China Lake. Of course, most people know about it only because of its dubious reputation for harboring scores of alien spacecraft in Area 51. One thing is for certain though: no one can get in, so the plane, the missile, and Lieutenant Colonel Alex Larson would be nearly impossible to trace.

Only Connor and the other members of the elite circle knew about flight plan number three.

The pilot did not.

***

All three generals and Colonel Olsen were at the conference table adjacent to General Bundy's office. Olsen was on his phone.

"Thank you, Major. Let me know if you run into any issues." He paused. "No, nothing expected. Thank you." He hung up and addressed them. "Larson took off at 2355 hours, three minutes ago."

A solemn silence hung in the room, as they were all acutely aware of the same dreadful thing at once. For those few moments, they were at a funeral.

Finally, Morrison spoke.

"It's a damn shame he can't be honored openly."

Olsen said sadly, "The whole thing is a damn shame. The world is coated with shame."

Bundy said, "Unfortunately, it's been that way for ages, Ed. At least this time we may be minutes away from preventing it from getting worse. In fact, if Larson succeeds, we have just a few minutes before the weapon unlocks. Then the kill window opens. Notify tech of his departure and get me a confirmation from Schuler that he is ready."

Olsen got on his phone again briefly, then hung up. "Confirmed, sir."

They waited.

Chapter 30

AIRBORNE

Mt. Whitney, California
November 4
12:10 a.m. (PDT)

Because the mission was inherently covert, there would be no communication after takeoff until Alex's approach at Groom Lake in Nevada. Visibility was good enough to fly VFR, visual flight rules. Even though a serious storm was moving in toward the Sierras, he would go in on the forward edge of it. At 450 miles per hour, the seventy-nine miles to the target would take only a few minutes. Alex reached up with his left hand toward a large toggle switch with three positions. Used for arming and disarming the weapon system, the switch was in the middle position, labeled Off. Down was Simulation. Up was Arm. Moments after he moved the lever up to arm the missiles, the weapons became available for use.

Targeting this missile is a technically complex but reasonably user-friendly process. A JASSM flies with layered guidance systems. On-board GPS, infrared, and 3d target identification allow the missile to locate and confirm the target by itself after launch. Of course, safety measures are built in. Under normal circumstances, a missile is not activated until after being released from the plane.

Tonight, however, circumstances for this mission were not normal, and unbeknownst to Alex, this point of safety had been set aside. The booby-trapped system had been re-programmed secretly to activate the second JASSM while it was still attached to the plane as if it too had been launched and was in flight. Everything was ready for the launch—much more so than the pilot knew.

During the next few minutes of the flight, Alex, still troubled by what he was about to do, began to muse about his birth father. *What would he have thought about this?* Then, without knowing why, part of that familiar song began to play in his mind, as it did sometimes; the Norwegian counting song from when he was a young child. He could never quite remember all of it, or if it meant anything. *Fem, seks, syv, atte, ni:* five, six, seven, eight, nine. He thought *It is odd what pops into your mind when you are about to blow up a cabin in the woods.*

Now it was time to divert from his current flight path— ostensibly toward Edwards Air Force Base—redirect to his target, then set up for launch. Alex veered left toward the target coordinates, which soon put him at the mouth of the canyon. He climbed to an altitude of 17,500 feet so he could launch the missile from a high position. After launch, he would descend very low across the top of the ridge and turn north, away from the area, using the incoming storm clouds for cover.

As the fighter closed in, to about four miles from the target, Alex drew his thumb up across the red Fire button at the upper part of the control stick and pressed it. The JASSM under his left wing detached, dropped, and began to carry out its flight profile.

Guided by the pre-programmed target coordinates, IR sensors, and 3d imaging, and propelled by a liquid fuel jet engine, the missile raced off toward the cabin. As with any air-to-air or air-to-ground missile, the electrical fuse waited for the weapon to be released to arm the warhead while in flight. With this weapon, not only would the cabin be flattened, but the remaining JP-8 kerosene would ignite in an air-fuel explosion, incinerating whatever was left in a spectacular blaze.

The launch was sequenced in the usual way, except for one detail, thanks to the ingenuity of the late Major Jim Barker. When the first missile was armed, it signaled the fuse mechanism of the unlaunched second weapon on the plane to do the same. Instead of being activated by normal targeting information, however, detonation was linked to a timer set for eight seconds.

Alex noticed an unusual reading on one of the other firing indicators, but before he could make sense of it, something else happened in that instant which was unexpected. A very large Canadian goose took a detour directly into the F-16's air intake. It had been flying in a V-formation with five other geese at the same altitude but moving in the opposite direction. The geese were seeking out a warmer climate as they migrated together—but not this warm. The bird strike produced an instant fire along with a loss of power and altitude.

Within four seconds, Alex made the decision. He was too low to experiment with the plane and attempt to regain power. He took hold of the yellow and black ejection handle directly in front of his seat and yanked it, hard. With about forty-five pounds of pull needed to activate the system, it required decisive action.

The next four seconds were, for Alex, expanded into a vivid, incredibly slow-motion video. The ejection rocket under his seat erupted, pushing the canopy away and the seat, with him in it, upward into the cold night. The air was not only frigid but hit him at nearly 450 miles per hour. His helmet came off. His left arm flew up and hit hard against the frame of the seat. The g-force and wind strength combined, coming from different directions, twisted his leg and strained a ligament in his knee. As he was propelled upward, he saw the fighter jet appear to drop downward, then—still in extreme slow-motion mode—he saw it explode below him in a massive fireball from the detonation of the remaining missile. He felt intense heat from the explosion gust across his face.

In those few moments, the shock wave from the explosion intensified every force. Alex knew he was losing blood pressure when his vision went gray. As he fought to remain conscious, he saw the chute open above him—but with a small section missing. Less than three seconds after ejecting from the exploding plane, it had deployed yet a little too close to the flames. Enough of the chute was still intact to slow his fall, but it began to spin, and Alex with it. His spinning gray vision went to black as he fell unconscious.

<u>Chapter 31</u>

A BUMP IN THE NIGHT

Mt. Whitney, California
November 4
12:12 a.m. (PDT)

"BOOM!" . . . . "BOOM!" Then very close, "CRASH!"

Two explosions, followed by the sound of something huge slamming into the side of the mountain near the road. The noise was loud enough to wake everyone at the campground. Boulder-sized rocks, dislodged by the impact, made a small avalanche, blocking the road. Fresh snow lying on the ground and in the trees reflected an orange-yellow light because part of the canyon higher up was ablaze.

Above the camp area, where Jason's cabin had been moments earlier, a fire was raging in the center of a ring of burning pine trees. The flames were beginning to spread outward and up the ridge.

Over the ridge to the north, the front half of the fighter jet had become wedged between two vertical rocks and was burning with bright orange flames, like a gigantic torch. The rest of the plane, with part of one wing still attached, lay at the bottom of the cliff at Mt.

McAdie, where it had fallen after crashing into it. Bits of metal and rubber showered down, littering the forest floor with debris—some of it on fire.

People poured out of their tents and cabins. Confused and fearful, everyone was groping for an explanation of what they had heard and for the fiery chaos.

Reggie sprang off his air mattress first, yelling, "What the hell is happening?!"

"Oh, God! This is it!" Sally had fallen asleep with Li Jing's "before time runs out" comment circulating in her mind.

When she and Reggie scrambled out of the tent and looked around, Sally was so relieved to learn that this was merely a catastrophic explosion.

People were looking up at the blaze, aghast. Pastor Kuan and his wife were checking each of the tents in space thirteen to see if people were okay. Children were crying. When all the people in the group had gathered in the middle of the campsite, Kuan said to them in a voice that was authoritative and steady, "I need your attention, everyone. It appears that an airplane has just crashed up on the hill. We need to be calm and take one step at a time. No one in our group is injured, so Larry and I are going to check with the other campers in a minute to see if anyone needs any help and we will report back here. Did anybody see it happen?"

Bob, a father in the group said, "I did. I was up walking in the snow and looking at the stars, and I heard a jet coming up the canyon. I turned to look over this way and saw a missile shoot out from it. Then the plane dove down pretty far, and when it got to right about there," pointing, "it burst into flames. Next thing I know, a ball of fire seemed to suck up that cabin on the top of the ridge, the one that sits on the big rock."

As they were leaving their campsite, Reggie and Sally walked toward Shen and Larry on the little road. Shen conveyed what he had just learned. Sally asked if he knew of any available communication link to the outside.

"The camp host has a satellite hook-up, so he should be able to get the news source."

Reggie commented, "That's good, but at this point, we are supposed to be the news source. Looks like we'll be writing a different kind of story now."

<u>Chapter 32</u>

FALLING

Mt. Whitney, California
November 4
12:12 a.m. (PDT)

When Alex's parachute opened, the seat fell away as per design; a life raft self-inflated, deployed, and dangled from a cord below him. Around the pilot's neck, a life vest filled with air. These are great features for ejecting over water, and it happened that Alex's life raft did touch down in water, with him next to it. Meysan Lake was in the canyon southwest of the target he had just destroyed and was made up of very cold snowmelt water.

Alex was unconscious when the cold rushed up his legs and torso, but by the time it got to his face, he sprang into consciousness with all the right questions: "Where? What? How?" It all came back to him within a few moments.

He surmised correctly that he had parachuted into a lake and that it was ice cold. Alex detested cold water. Meanwhile, the ejection seat had splashed down into the far side of the lake.

Frigid water, unpleasant as it was, may have been what his knee and wrist needed. However, he was starting to feel the pain and stiffness everywhere. The trauma of being hurled out of a plane into a 450-mile-per-hour blast of wind, jerked up by a parachute, then flung into a cold lake threatened to outweigh the good news that he was still alive. He felt very sleepy. Shock was setting in—but there was no time for that. With all the willpower he could muster, he forced the lethargic feeling aside and commanded himself into action.

Considering that the impossible had just happened—a missile exploding before it was even fired—Alex was not in a trusting mood. It was clear that someone had intended to kill him. He decided to let them think they had succeeded.

While he was still in the water, he detached the parachute harness from himself, gathered and rolled up the chute, then stuffed it in his small life raft. After that, he swam twenty or so yards with it to the closest shore. Once he had rested for nearly a full minute, he gathered a few good-sized rocks and piled them on top of the chute inside the raft. After tossing a small backpack containing survival items, onto the shore, he summoned the nerve to swim back out in the frigid water with the inflated raft, far enough to sink it safely out of sight, then punctured it before swimming back to shore.

As soon as he touched the shore, his body began to shiver. For survival, his priorities now were warmth and concealment. Included in the survival kit that followed him out of the cockpit was an assortment of supplies: a big knife that he had just used, matches, a small flashlight, something that approximated food, etc. Some pilots carry personal weapons according to their own preferences. Alex was accustomed to keeping a 9mm Sig P226 with him in combat environments, but he also carried it as a matter of habit whenever he flew.

About thirty yards away from the edge of the lake was a grouping of gigantic boulders leaning against each other. Behind one of them, he found the remains of an old campfire partially covered with snow. With his knife, he cleared it out, then scrounged for small pieces of burnable wood. Grateful for the waterproof matches in the pack, Alex converted the wood he found into a small fire under the visual cover of the boulders. More snow was falling. His hands were getting numb.

***

The three generals and Colonel Olsen sat at the conference table in General Bundy's office, waiting for news about the mission. Olsen's phone rang.

An urgent voice on the other end said, "Colonel, regarding the two missiles you wanted me to track. I have some bad news, sir. They never made it to Edwards. Shortly after he took off, Lieutenant Colonel Larson diverted from his flight plan, flew into a canyon in the Sierras, and fired on a civilian resort cabin. The report I have here says he fired the two missiles he was transporting, then flew himself into a cliff. It's hard to believe, sir, but that's the intel I have. A damage control team and a tanker have been deployed."

"This is very bad news, Major," Olsen replied. "Thank you, we'll take it from here."

He hung up and said, "The first report is that Larson completed his mission. Both missiles went off and, of course, they think he fired them both. The damage control team has been deployed. It looks like he did it. The DNA should be wiped out. Our kill window is now open."

Bundy said, "Notify Schuler. We are unlocked and he is cleared to use the device. Remind him to start with Kasym Nazarov. It's about 1500 hours in Almaty. His girlfriend, Ayana, will be getting home soon. She knows to tell her Facebook friend, Inkar, if there is any news about him, like death. Either way, she checks in every night before bed. As soon as we get confirmation from Ayana that Nazarov is dead, we go down the list."

Chapter 33

SUSPICIOUSLY PREPARED

Mt. Whitney, California
November 4
12:43 a.m. (PDT)

Thirty-one minutes after the two missiles exploded, flames were spreading from where the cabin had been; however, the fire was moving mostly uphill. Dropping temperatures and new snow helped slow the advance of the fire, but still, it was moving. To the north, what looked like a passenger jet turned toward the mouth of the canyon at a very low altitude, toward the fire. Initially, most of the campers were alarmed, wondering if this night would ever be over. What happened next, though, put them at ease.

The plane was one of the DC-10s that had been converted for use as an air tanker. It could deliver thousands of gallons of fire suppressant to a site in one pass. From its low position, the tanker climbed gently upward, releasing a huge quantity of red liquid directly on and along the ridge where most of the fire was—an impressive maneuver. This was the second plane that night to hit its target—the same target. One more trip and the major fires would be stopped.

Smaller fires from pieces of burning debris were being tracked down by Forest Service workers who had been asleep in bed just a little while ago.

Turning to Larry, Shen Kuan said, "Have you ever seen a tanker like that loaded and at a fire within thirty minutes?"

Larry replied, "Only in a drill—when it was not a surprise."

"Does all this look like a surprise to you?" asked Shen.

"Nope," said Larry.

Shen and Larry continued to go around the campground looking for people who needed help, both physical and emotional. About an hour and a half later, they headed back to their campsite. Coming up the road toward them were two men dressed in camo fatigues, carrying clipboards. They were questioning people about what they had seen.

"Hi, I'm Lieutenant Martinez and this is Sergeant Nelson. We are investigating this incident. Did either of you see what happened?"

Larry answered, "We were asleep when it happened but, when we heard it, we could tell it was a problem with a plane."

Martinez asked further, "Did anyone happen to mention seeing the pilot eject?"

"No. But a member of our group said he thought he saw the plane fire a missile and hit that cabin up there. I didn't see it, though," said Shen.

Larry said, "Lieutenant, I have a few questions for you—like, how it is that a United States Air Force jet fires on a civilian target inside this country? Can you tell us anything about this?"

Martinez said, "Not much. We are in the process of getting the facts straight."

Just then, a helicopter flew directly overhead toward Mt. McAdie, where a large piece of the F-16 had fallen. The chopper disappeared over the ridge.

Looking up, Martinez said, "That's part of our team. We need to head that way now, but when we come back, can you direct me to the person who says he saw a missile being fired?"

"Okay," said Shen.

"Thank you, gentlemen."

They both hurried off as if to shorten the conversation.

"Surprised, Shen?"

"Not entirely," he said. "It reminds me of my home."

"How is that?" asked Larry.

"Back home, I saw my government break the law, then say they did not know about it. They would ask us questions but would not answer questions. So much was happening, always behind a curtain, but few were brave enough to pull the curtain back for all to see."

Chapter 34

A NEW ROOMMATE

Mt. Whitney, California
November 4
12:12 a.m. (PDT)

Jason was a light sleeper. Plus, the cot he used in the Quonset hut shelter was a little uneven and not padded. Whenever he stayed at the hut, he used one of the sleeping bags stored there, but he never felt cold enough to need more than that. It was cozy and private. The low clouds and fresh layer of snow on the ground and over the hut made it very quiet.

Shortly after midnight, he awakened to the sound of a boom, low and muffled, but still powerful. Then another one, this time louder. Both were stronger and deeper than the sound of a deer rifle.

That couldn't have been a gun, he thought. *Besides, who would be shooting in the middle of the night? It must have been jets from China Lake making sonic booms. It was so loud though. They were probably flying way too low.*

As quickly as he could, he put on his boots and jacket and went outside to investigate. A very short walk up the trail, there was a place that overlooked Meysan Lake.

Clouds were rolling in and it was getting colder. Normally, it would have been a lot darker, but the snow on the ground and in the trees reflected and enhanced the available light. After surveying the lake area from the overlook, he walked a few more yards up the trail to get a slightly better view. But all he could see was raw, now quiet, snow-wrapped beauty. Nothing unusual for that place. It started to snow, and Jason went back into the shelter, still wondering what that noise might have been.

About fifteen minutes later, he went back out for another look. This time, he noticed a small tail of smoke rising from behind some large boulders on the side of the lake closest to him, but no light. Long ago, the big rocks had broken off from above and fallen, clearing their own path before they came to a halt together beside where the lake was now. After watching for a minute or so, he decided to go down there and check it out in case someone needed help. Jason locked the door of the hut behind him and set off for the lake.

When he got to the place where he saw the smoke, he noticed a few footprints in the snow, but no people. One of three huge boulders was leaning against the other two, forming a low entrance to a natural space between them which was partially open at the top. He stooped down and went in. At the center of the space was a very small, smoldering fire. It was covered with snow and making a lot of smoke as if someone had recently tried to put it out. Jason walked over to it and kicked over one of the charred pieces. Then, he heard a voice.

"On your face!"

As he turned his head to the left, where the voice came from, he could only see the muzzle of a handgun protruding from a shadow about six feet away. Fear splashed throughout his body, and for a moment, he felt paralyzed.

"Do it now!" said the voice from the shadow.

"Okay, okay!" Jason hit the ground, lying face-first in the snow.

The voice demanded, "Who are you?"

"Jason Greer, Forest Service. I saw smoke and thought someone might be in trouble."

"Oh yeah—what are you doing up here in the middle of the night?" said the voice.

"I came up here earlier, warning people about a storm tonight. It was too late to make it back to my cabin, so I decided to stay overnight," said Jason.

"Overnight where?"

Not wanting to reveal where the shelter was, but at the same time wishing to stay alive, Jason deflected the question. "You mind telling me who you are and how come you are here? Look, if you're okay camping here, I can go. Otherwise, maybe I can help if you need it."

The person in the dark ignored his question. "I assume you have I.D. on you. Throw it over here."

Still lying on his face in the cold, Jason wrestled his trembling hand to his back pocket, took out his wallet, and tossed it into the shadows toward the voice. Then, he realized he had just given his wallet to a stranger with a weapon.

"Idiot," said Jason out loud.

"Watch your mouth, buddy," said the other. "I'm the one with a gun here."

"I didn't mean you—sorry," said Jason.

Then a man stepped out of the shadow, squinting at the driver's license. "So, if you are Jason Greer, then what's your social?"

The man's tone reminded Jason of the highway patrolman who

had given him a speeding ticket two weeks earlier. However, he pushed that thought aside, trying to remember the number. "Uh . . . 405-92-20 . . . uh . . ."

The man interrupted, "Close enough—I can't see it very well anyway. You can get up now. Is anyone with you?"

"Just me," he said, getting up. "I tend to go it alone."

Jason had expected to see a rustic, fur-covered, smelly mountain-dweller with an old western-style revolver, or even a drifting vagrant who robbed people for drug money. Instead, a formidable-looking guy with a recent haircut and a sopping wet flight suit stood there shivering and pointing a newer-style weapon.

Meanwhile, Alex continued to watch the forest ranger closely, unwilling to trust him fully, though he seemed harmless. He wondered if there was anyone he could trust after what he had been through.

"So, you fell in the lake?" Jason asked.

"Landed," Alex said.

Jason glanced at the oak leaf patch on Alex's sleeve. "Lieutenant Colonel?"

"Right. I hit a bird and ejected into the damn water," said Alex.

"I see. So, why are you pointing that gun at me?" asked Jason.

"There are people who apparently want me dead," said Alex. "I want to be sure you're not one of them. You said you were staying somewhere. Where?" He was shivering almost convulsively now.

"I'll show you. It's a shelter for emergencies," said Jason. "You'll be able to warm up there and get some food and dry clothes."

"All right. Some rangers carry guns, right? I need to see that you are unarmed."

Slowly, Jason opened his jacket, patted himself down awkwardly, and turned all the way around to demonstrate that he was not carrying a weapon.

"I don't usually carry a gun with me," said Jason.

"Ankles."

To show him there was no holster, Jason pulled up the cuff on each ankle. Alex seemed satisfied.

"That's good enough. Let's go." Alex kicked more snow over the last of the embers and they began walking up the trail, Jason leading the way and Alex still holding his gun with numb fingers. About a quarter of a mile later, they turned off-trail to the left and started up a hill. After a few more minutes of climbing, they came to the hut. Mostly covered with leaning bows of pine trees and fresh snow, it was almost completely camouflaged.

Inside, Jason lit a propane stove sitting on a small table. Alex sat in a chair, laid his weapon on the table next to the stove, and began warming his hands over the rising heat. Jason poured water from a jug into a teapot and put it on the second burner. A cardboard box sat next to the door with a miscellaneous collection of shirts, pants, jackets, and shoes. Jason brought the box over to Alex, then opened the door of a small cabinet by the stove and began looking for something to feed his guest.

"You'll be able to warm up with some coffee soon," said Jason.

"Thanks." Alex could see that Jason was what he appeared to be, but enough had challenged his sense of reality lately that he was being particularly careful.

"Pop Tart?" Jason tossed a packet to him. "Strawberry."

"You eat this crap?" said Alex.

"Look at the label. Fruit. It's good for you, especially if you are freezing to death."

They both snickered a little. Alex finally returned his pistol to its holster.

"Should I call you sir, or what?" asked Jason.

"Alex is fine."

After some food and warmth, as well as a set of dry clothes, they spoke more. Alex coaxed Jason to talk about himself, wanting to keep the conversation one-sided. Jason told about how he became a ranger, about his sister in Lone Pine, and that he lived in one of the thirty or so cabins in the Portal area.

"Which one—er, I mean, how high up is it?" asked Alex. In preparation for the strike, he had become familiar with the area, and he wondered how far away Jason's place might be from the one he had just destroyed.

"It's the highest one on the ridge—sits on a big rock outcropping. Beautiful view."

Alex did his best to hide his disbelief, staring at him for a stunned moment, then turning his eyes to his coffee cup as he took a sip. Possibilities and suspicions flooded his mind. His thoughts raced. *That cabin was the target! Is Jason somehow involved with the weapon I was sent to destroy? Is he oblivious? He acts like he does not even know about the air strike. Who is this guy?*

"Anything unusual about the place?" asked Alex.

"A lot. For one, it stays warm all winter. No joke, and I don't know why. The rock it sits on seems to have its own heat. I checked it out and learned that the guy who built it was a scientist from Norway. He worked out of China Lake for a while before he died."

"Did you get his name?" asked Alex, trying to keep a casual tone.

"Sundheim. Soren Sundheim."

Adrenaline spiked in Alex's bloodstream, but he did not dare show it. Hearing his birth father's name in the middle of this situation was paralyzing.

"Anything else odd about the place?" he asked as casually as possible.

Jason said, "Here is something unusual. Inside the hall closet, there is a second door panel, with another smaller closet behind that.

I found these boots and this parka there, left behind by a previous owner, I guess. Both are really good quality but old. The nice thing is that they are a perfect fit for me."

Connor's words about a fearful weapon related to the cabin suddenly came back to Alex, as if he were there with them: "It involves the DNA of the son of a bitch who built it!"

Alex's mind raced, both discovering and trying to push back a realization at the same time. He thought, *My real father's DNA must be all over this Jason guy's boots and parka. This is his parka! They tried to destroy it, and me—my DNA too? That's why Connor insisted it had to be me flying this mission. Damn Connor—liar! 'Chosen because of my character'—and I believed it!*

Alex was formulating what he would say next when they heard the tiny sound of a text notification. Jason looked at his phone and saw over twenty texts from his sister, which he had not noticed. "Jason, call me." "Jason, call me now!" "Jason! This is Jeanie. If you are alive, please call me!"

"This is weird, my sister is trying to reach me—something important. She can be so dramatic, though." He dialed her back.

"Do not say anything about me!" said Alex with a commanding tone.

"Right. Hi, Jeanie, what's happening?" He listened in silence for about thirty seconds. Alex could hear a faint telephone voice going on excitedly about something. He watched the expression on Jason's face morph from surprise, shock, anger, and grief, as if he was hearing some crushing news—because he was.

"No, I'm just fine. Sorry you were scared. Okay, I'll do better at answering my text messages. Look, don't get mad. I know it was scary. Listen, I'll call you back in a few minutes." He ended the call, dazed by the conversation.

Jason and Alex stared at each other, eye to eye in total silence, for another ten full seconds. Jason imagined the cabin going up in flames along with the hopeful direction his life had been taking, his future, everything. Alex could see the turmoil in Jason's eyes.

"Sorry about your cabin," said Alex.

Jason shouted angrily, "You destroyed it?!"

"Completely. Believe me, there is nothing left," Alex replied.

"My sister said it started a forest fire!"

"I would think so," said Alex calmly.

"Then she said a tanker came by within thirty minutes and put it out," Jason said, still getting used to the reality of the discovery.

"That figures," Alex said.

Jason shouted, "That was my house! It's where I lived, you know! Why did you blow it up, damn it?!"

With some reluctance, Alex said, "That's a little difficult to answer."

"I think you owe it to me!" said Jason angrily.

Alex decided that, since they were both now in mortal danger from the same people, it would be better if Jason knew more. He told him he had been sent to destroy that building by some nefarious people who convinced him it contained something that constituted a national and even international threat. It had something to do with DNA and a weapon that had to be destroyed. Alex did not reveal what he had realized about the parka and boots Jason was wearing— that they might be carrying some of the DNA in question as well.

"A weapon—at the cabin?" said Jason, perplexed.

"They wouldn't give me details, but I have a good idea now. I probably shouldn't have gone along with it," Alex said pensively.

Jason shouted, "You think!?" Then, calming himself down, he added, "We need to find out more. My sister just said she and a friend of hers have some information about what may be going on here. She insists on meeting so they can tell me what they know."

"Does she know where this place is?" asked Alex.

"Yes," said Jason, "I showed it to her last year. She and I call it 'that place.'"

"How many other people know about it?"

Jason was becoming calm now. "Only a few locals and some other rangers who are in the field during summer. We keep it low-key."

Alex said, "Get her back on the phone and see if she'll come here. We need information. Can she keep all this to herself? This is serious, and we don't need drama. Also, she can't know I'm here until she arrives."

"Oh yeah, she is solid," said Jason. "The drama I mentioned was brother-sister stuff."

"Okay," said Alex. "If she has a vehicle, tell her she has to park it away from this shelter and hide it. Also, tell her to turn back if she sees anyone following her."

Jason called Jeanie back. "Jeanie, listen, I only have a minute. I need you to meet me at 'that place' as soon as you can. You are right, we need to compare notes." He paused, listening. "Okay, bring her with you if you need to, but no one else can know. This is serious. You'll have to use Keven's Sidewinder. He's in San Diego but the key is above the south window frame in his garage. Hook up the trailer and take Olivas Ranch Road. Turn off toward the canyon and keep going until you hit snow, then drive the Sidewinder from there. And be sure to put gas in it." He paused again. "All right, okay. Of course, you would, I was just reminding you. Okay, thanks. I love you too, sis. Me too, I'm glad I'm alive too. Also, call me if you need to but not if you don't. Okay, I'll watch for texts. Park a good distance away from here, cover the snowmobile up, and walk the rest of the way. Hey, also, if you think someone is following you, turn back and text me. See ya." Jason hung up.

"Bring who?" said Alex.

"Her friend. She's a nurse and she was married to a military guy named Barker who may have had something to do with this. He died mysteriously in July. She and my sister met at a church she goes to. They've been trying to figure out what her husband was up to since he was killed," said Jason.

"The name is familiar," said Alex. "Does he have a technical background?"

Jason answered, "Maybe. I'm not sure. You can ask her when she gets here."

<u>Chapter 35</u>

THE FAST-TRACK UPHILL

Lone Pine, California
November 4
4:30 a.m. (PDT)

Jeanie hung up after talking with Jason and immediately called Katie Barker. A short summary was enough.

"I don't have time for more details, but I need you to meet me at Keven Bales' house. We are going to borrow his snowmobile," said Jeanie.

Hooking up the trailer was not too hard. Jeanie had done it before with Keven, who was Jason's good friend. After stopping briefly for gas, they were on the road. Hearing that Jason was alive was good news, and that he had information to share was even better.

From Olivas Ranch Road, the view was a sobering sight. High on the ridge to their right, plumes of gray smoke rose from the extinguished fire. As they were driving across the foothill area, everything was painted white by a light covering of snow. They continued beyond where the road became dirt. After a mile or more, the truck tires began to slip in the icy mud. Jeanie pulled to the side of the road to unload the snowmobile. Keven had bought it new at the end of last season and had only used it a few times. It had been sitting all summer, but he always kept the battery charged.

They let the short ramp down at the back of the trailer. Then Jeanie got on the snowmobile, inserted the ignition key, and the Yamaha fired up. She had to drive it off the trailer because it was too heavy to push. After she eased it down the ramp to the ground, she remembered to call her husband and tell him where he could retrieve the truck and trailer. He would be returning that day from a work trip to San Francisco.

Katie got on the snowmobile behind Jeanie, and they started out.

After becoming accustomed to the instant power, almost falling off, then having to circle back to retrieve a pair of loose sunglasses, they sped off up the mountain.

Katie yelled, "I forgot to ask. Do you know where you are going?"

"Yes, but it's pretty well hidden."

***

In General Bundy's office, Colonel Olsen hung up the phone again. "Ayana responded to Inkar on her Facebook with a lot of mundane crap about her day and what a rude bastard Nazarov was with her tonight."

Bundy was astonished. "Nazarov is alive? Damn! What could have happened?"

Connor said, "There is no question that the building was incinerated. What about the plane?"

Morrison added, "The report I got from the ground is that the plane broke up and the pieces were in flames."

"Was the ejection seat fired?" asked Bundy.

Olsen said, "It was impossible to tell upon first inspection, sir, but no one has spotted a chute or the seat anywhere in that canyon or the one next to it, and there is no beacon signal."

"See how long it will take for Dr. Schuler to detect the DNA signatures again," said Bundy. "If Larson is alive, then we'll know what the problem is—and the solution. He must be eliminated from the equation."

"Yes, sir," Olsen replied.

Chapter 36

THE MORNING NEWS

Bishop, California
November 4
7:00 a.m. (PDT)

Steve Owens and Lina Sherman were co-anchors for Foothills
Cable News in Bishop, California. As they did each day, they were
presenting the morning news. Steve began with a breaking story.

"Campers vacationing in the Mt. Whitney Portal area, just
off 395 Highway near Lone Pine, had a rude awakening just after
midnight. Witnesses say what appeared to be an F-16 fighter jet flew
into the canyon and destroyed one of the cabins in the area. Two of
our affiliate reporters are on the scene. They tell us that, so far, there
are two versions of the incident. Some say the jet fired a missile that
hit the structure; then, seconds later, the plane exploded in a ball of
flames. Others say the pilot lost control and crashed into the cabin,
setting it and the surrounding forest on fire."

Lina joined in, "Speaking of fire, the response from the aerial
fire team was impressive to say the least. A single tanker carrying fire

retardant arrived on the scene less than thirty minutes after the blaze started. Between the tanker and the dedicated firefighters on the ground, we can be grateful the fire is nearly contained."

Steve continued, "The Forest Service reports that ten inches of snow cover from the night before, along with the absence of any adverse winds, helped them get things under control. The timing of these things can be very uncanny."

Lina added, "Yes, it can. Presently, no one seems to know the real cause of the incident or the name of the pilot. Additionally, we are waiting to learn if anyone was in the structure which was destroyed in the blast. We will keep you informed."

Steve added, "Meanwhile, the CHP and the Forest Service are asking that people stay away from the area as much as possible until the incident can be better understood. Additionally, no one can enter or leave the campground at present because of a road blockage due to falling debris."

"As this unusual story unfolds," said Lina, "no doubt, you will hear different things from multiple sources. Already, there are many versions of what happened on the internet. However, you can rely on us as your most reliable news source. As always, we will keep you up to date."

***

Lina was right. The energy released by the two exploding missiles was small compared to the firestorm on the internet, where people with every possible perspective were certain they had the inside story.

Many virtual enemies were made that day. Pundits declared who the guilty party was—opinions ricocheted from the pilot to the government, both deep and shallow states, foreign states, those who endanger our natural forests, and back again to the personalities of our leaders. A few of the theories were accidentally close, but no one really knew the truth. Only eleven people fully understood what was at stake—yet even they were unaware that time was running out in a much different way.

Chapter 37

UNDERCOVER MANHUNT

China Lake, California
November 4
7:15 a.m. (PDT)

All four officers continued their vigil in General Bundy's office. Olsen's phone rang yet again. "Yes, Dr. Schuler, we are all here, waiting for your call." He listened for a few moments, then said, "Okay, thank you. Keep trying to refine the location. We will keep you posted too." He hung up.

Olsen reported, "Schuler says there are still two energy signatures, but they are so weak they can't be pinpointed. It must mean Larson is still alive. Schuler says the signal is very distorted, though, so it will take a hell of a long time to be exact about the location. This is not the same as getting a simple GPS coordinate. Since the signal is not dependent on space, the location in space has to be surmised. It takes time."

Signs of fatigue showed on the faces of the four men. They had been up all night, waiting for the "kill window" to open. Of course, their best intention behind the "kill" part was to save the world from a tyrannical inevitability should the six despotic people on the other side of the globe be allowed to live.

In the mental space often created by simply having to wait, it occurred to Olsen that, in their urgency to be the first ones to unlock the device, they may have neglected an important issue.

He said to Bundy, "General, I have a question about relocking the weapon. I think we all agree that after using it this one time, it should be locked permanently from being used by anyone, ever. Have you spoken to Schuler recently about how we will do that? For instance, would he use DNA to block it the way Sundheim did?"

Bundy replied, "Schuler is looking for options. However, he told me Sundheim's method of using his own DNA to lock the weapon made it too vulnerable to being unlocked. Eliminate one or two people and it's ready to use. He says if we plan to lock it up permanently, one way would be to link it with the genome of an entire race of people, one that is established. No one could use the weapon unless they were all eliminated. He thinks that would make it secure."

Olsen thought, but was too reluctant to say: *What if some evil lunatic tried to eliminate a whole race in order to get that kind of power? It's been tried before.*

Morrison said, "Either way, for now, we have to locate Larson. He must have ejected before the plane was destroyed, so he has to be somewhere in that area. We need to get agents down there now. Anybody know if he is armed?"

"He always carries a pistol," said Connor.

"What about the AR-15 in the ejection kit?" asked Morrison.

"No, we included only the minimum in his kit," said Connor.

"Okay. Tell the agents to present themselves as Forest Service people. However, they will be hunting an armed fugitive. He is to be killed on sight, no questions, but they are to make it look as if he was trying to escape or that he was endangering someone."

Olsen responded, "We have three agents who can do that, sir."

"Also, no one leaves that canyon until I clear it. Damage assessment shows boulders and part of the plane are blocking the road now, so we need to leave it that way for a while. Everyone stays in the area until we find him. Let people know that we need to complete our investigation first and that there may be a criminal issue, so no one can leave yet. Have the Forest Service provide for anyone in the canyon until we are done so no one creates a problem."

Chapter 38

STARTLING DISCOVERIES

Mt. Whitney, California
November 4
7:15 a.m. (PDT)

Jeanie and Katie continued up the canyon that lies parallel to the one where the road was blocked by the rock avalanche. Jason's cabin had been on the ridge between the two canyons. Jeanie had come this way before, but now that the area was covered with snow, it looked a little different. Using the Sidewinder in the snow meant that a trail was not essential, but it helped.

Before intersecting the Meysan Trail, they first had to make their way upward through forest and snow to the top of the ridge, where the elevation was over 3,000 feet higher than where they left the truck. Then, they traveled about six more miles, and another 3,000 feet higher, on or near the trail toward the lake and the shelter. In the frigid wind, it became a very long ride.

Finally, they got to about fifty or so yards from the shelter. Jeanie drove the vehicle as far into a bush as she could to conceal it, then turned off the engine. Working together, Jeanie and Katie piled pine branches and snow over it, then started walking toward the hut. As Jason had warned, they tried their best to keep an eye out for anyone following them. However, with senses dulled from the cold and a rough ride, they were unaware that they were being observed.

When Jeanie saw Jason standing outside the shelter, she ran and hugged him, tears freezing on her face. "Oh, Jason, I'm so glad to see you."

"I'm glad to see you too," said Jason. "Good job getting here."

"I'm so sorry about your cabin," said Jeanie.

"That's what he said," replied Jason, pointing to a man standing about ten feet behind Katie and Jeanie. Alex had just stepped into the clearing.

"Whoa! Who is this?" exclaimed Jeanie, startled.

"This is Lieutenant Colonel Alex Larson. He's the one who incinerated the cabin," said Jason.

Dumbfounded, she stared at Alex for more than a few seconds, the way he and her brother had done earlier.

In his change of clothes, Alex did not look military but more like a guy who did not know how to shop for himself. For him, this was good because he wanted to be incognito.

Jeanie stammered, "I don't understand. But wait, maybe I do."

Suddenly, Jeanie realized how Alex fit into all this. A surge of energy rose up within her. Her voice turned to anger, "Did you shoot a missile into my brother's house?!"

"Yes, ma'am," said Alex.

"Why?! Who do you think—" As she was about to lay into him, Jason, stepped in front of her and said calmly, "We have a lot to talk about. Let's go inside and thaw out."

Inside, there was hot coffee and food for the two women, and they began to warm up. Likewise, Jeanie began to cool off.

Jason said to Alex, "This is my sister, Jeanie."

"I gathered that," said Alex.

Jeanie said, "This is Katie, my friend."

Jason began explaining how he had come to the shelter rather than going home the night before, narrowly missing death, and how he met Alex, who had nearly died as well.

"When the Colonel and I—"

"Alex," said Alex.

"Okay," continued Jason. "When Alex and I discussed this situation, we realized we were missing information that we desperately need, some of which you both may have. So, now we need to put all of it on the table and decide what to do."

Alex began, "Bottom line, the only reason I'm able to talk with you about this is that I'm very sure I am being targeted by my own people and it looks like each of us here has part of the whole picture.

"I was sent here to destroy Jason's cabin. It had something to do with DNA that was there and a weapon. I was not told who owned it, but I was assured the building would be empty. Shortly after I fired the first missile, the second missile exploded on the aircraft, which, by the way, never happens. It was sabotage. However, I got out in time, thanks to God I guess, when a bird flew up my air intake at the right moment. Then, I parachuted into that lake over there. That's where I ran into Jason."

Katie was curious. "A bird?"

"It was big; maybe a goose."

Then Jeanie described what they had learned about Jason's cabin: that it was built by a Norwegian physicist named Sundheim and that he had been working at China Lake on a thermal transfer project of some kind. She added that he was killed in a fire on a ship near the Arctic Sea.

Katie related her experience as Jim Barker's wife and the

information she gleaned from his rants. She talked about her suspicions regarding his death, learning that the coroner was fake and that the investigators had done little, not even considering her as a likely suspect.

She said, "Jim was especially angry about someone named Connor who put him in a compromising position. He said they expected him to show his loyalty to his country by helping to kill an innocent man. Supposedly, it was to prevent something more terrible from happening. It was about DNA and a weapon of some kind that would let someone control all the governments of the world."

Alex asked, "Did General Connor say what Jim was supposed to do?"

"General Brian Connor?" she asked.

"Yes—you know about him?"

"I only heard the last name from Jim, but Jeanie's husband researched all the Connors at China Lake and this general's name came up along with the others. So, it must be the one you know."

"Right," he replied.

"Jim once said something about 'jerry-rigging a booby-trap missile'," said Katie.

Alex said, "I've heard of Jim Barker but never met him. He was a Marine with an engineering background, but he also had a special knack for intelligence issues that were classified. It looks like Connor enlisted him to work on my plane."

Katie asked, "What do you mean?"

Alex explained, "Someone who knew a lot technically found a way to override the safety measures of the second missile I was carrying so it would blow my plane up after I fired the first one. My birth father's name was Soren Sundheim, so you could say I have his DNA. He is the one who built the cabin. I'm supposed to be dead."

Katie, finally understanding the mystery, lowered her head and began sobbing into her hands. Before her stood the innocent man her deceased husband had alluded to, the one he'd been assigned to kill. Jeanie came over, sat beside her, and embraced her silently. Then Jeanie began praying with her. At first, the men watched in silence.

Jason explained to Alex, "Jeanie has been trying to help Katie figure this out for months and I guess now it all makes sense. They met at Jeanie's church after Jim Barker was killed. Jeanie shared with Katie about her faith, and she became a believer too. Now they pray together sometimes and study the Bible and such."

"Good for them," said Alex.

"So, you too?"

"Yeah, but I haven't talked with God in a while. I slammed the door on Him when something, well, terrible happened. I get how Katie is overwhelmed by the evil of it, but I do know God is involved somehow. He's always doing a hell of a lot of good in the middle of the bad stuff."

"A hell of a lot of good?"

"Well, look at us. We should both be dead. If you had stayed home, you would be gone. If my plane hadn't sucked in a bird right then, I would be too. There's no way all this is a coincidence."

"Yeah, but how can you know for sure?"

"Maybe that's the faith part," Alex said. "Definitely there are coincidences. But when they stack up and they keep stacking up facing a certain direction, there's a point where you have to say maybe there is something spiritual going on that you can't see. Sometimes you just know it's true, even if you don't like it."

"Yeah, I've had that happen for sure."

Katie and Jeanie, listening in now from across the room, were astonished to realize that Alex understood.

Jason said, "How did you come to see things this way?"

"My adoptive dad," said Alex. "He told me he learned a lot from a Norwegian physicist friend. I just realized today that it was my original father he was talking about. Anyway, whatever you decide to do with faith is up to you. For now, though, we all need to decide what we are going to do because if the people who blew up my plane realize I got out alive, I expect them to be coming after me. It will be best if we all separate."

Jason said, "Not me. I'm not splitting up. You need to stay alive, especially if killing you has something to do with using some bizarre weapon. I think you made a crappy decision when you went along with the assignment to wreck my place, but what the hell—it looks like something bigger is happening here."

Jeanie, still listening in, said, "Jason's right. I'm not splitting up either."

Katie added, "Me neither."

Alex said, "Hold on—you should all think about this. If you get identified with me, it's a sure thing they will kill you too. They cannot afford for anyone to know what they are doing, or about this weapon they are playing with."

Katie said, "All those in favor of staying, say 'aye.'"

All three said, "Aye."

"You are stuck with us, Admiral," joked Katie.

"All right then," said Alex. "Looks like there's no changing your minds, at least for now. Thank you. Now, even if there really is a weapon like this—I mean one that depends on my DNA being destroyed—I'm not volunteering to die so Connor can save the world or whatever he is trying to do with it. I knew him. We fought together. However, since then, he has changed, and now I don't trust him at all."

Jason said, "It looks like we have two options. One is, we find a way to make you disappear. That way, at least, we can delay them from using their weapon, maybe permanently. Otherwise, we help you isolate Connor somehow, make him talk, and go from there."

Jeanie interjected, "We shouldn't be hasty. What if we go to the next canyon and get more information about what they are doing and see what military people are there? We come back here at the end of the day and decide what to do next."

Katie added, "She's right. We need to know what we are up against out there."

"The amount of time we have depends on when they figure out that I'm still alive, but this plan sounds good. Okay," said Alex.

Since there had been no word from Jason yet to the world outside, it was generally assumed that he had died when his cabin was destroyed. They all decided to prolong his anonymity by leaving him behind to guard the hut and work on hiding it a little better. The others would take the Sidewinder to just below the top of the ridge on this side but above the Portal Campground. Then, they would hide it and split up. Jeanie would hike over to the store at the end of the road, become friendly with people there, and see what they knew. Alex and Katie would go down and take a walk through the campground, then back up the hill to see how close they could get to the activity at the cabin. At 1600 hours they would all meet at the Sidewinder and head back to the shelter from there.

Jeanie whispered to Katie, "What is 1600 hours?"

Katie responded, "Four o'clock."

Jeanie smiled. "Got it. Roger. Over."

Alex took Jason's green knit stocking cap with the big Forest Service shield on the front flap and a pair of sunglasses he found in the hut. At least he could say he was a Forest Service worker if he needed to. He could turn it inside out if the disguise was not necessary. He also found a heavy blue jacket with decent insulation and another set of clothes, just in case.

Jason came over and handed Alex a pair of gloves. "Here, you'll need these. I bought them last year and they're pretty warm. There is another pair of socks in there too."

Alex said, "Thanks, Jason. Too bad you don't have a gun."

"Oh, I have one here," replied Jason. "It's a 45-caliber 1911. It's in a little floor safe here in the hut. I decided to start carrying it in case I run into a rabid bear."

"You have rabid bears here?" asked Alex.

"I've never actually seen one," answered Jason, "but I'm being more careful. Who wants to die foaming at the mouth?"

"Not me," said Alex. "All right, keep it with you. Remember, if anybody shoots at you after we leave, shoot back."

"Right," Jason replied.

Alex and the two women hiked over to where the Sidewinder was hidden and cleared off the camouflage. With Alex as pilot, they took off for the Portal area. Although the vehicle was not made for three people, it was powerful and could do the job easily. They arrived at the end of the ridge in just under an hour.

Chapter 39

A FAILING GRADE

Almaty, Kazakhstan
November 4
10:15 p.m. (ALMT)
14 Hours Ahead of California

"Come in."

Salamat Tursyn stepped into Tamir Abilov's office, a little nervous about interrupting him. At the same time, he was certain Abilov would want to hear what he had to say.

"We received a ULF message we thought you would want to see. Curiously, it is coded in Arabic, but we are getting closer to deciphering it. None of us are familiar with Arabic, so we found a Jewish rabbi who was a professor in linguistics. As a political dissident, he is in prison for his activities. However, he is known for his ability to interpret ancient texts."

"What does he say?"

"According to him, the message is made up of two Arabic words, one of them used twice. Both words have the same consonants, yet they can be used as either nouns or verbs. This man claims to understand the meaning."

"What is the meaning?"

"First, there is a cryptic reference to an ancient scale that weighs something, like when people would weigh money to see if it fits the standard of weight for a purchase. The word, 'mene', used twice, indicates that we have been weighed on a scale. The third word is 'tekel'. It indicates that we are lacking somehow. We have been weighed and it has been determined that we are lacking. The rabbi said that part of the code consists in how the letters are arranged."

"Lacking what? Where does this transmission come from?"

"This one is very unusual, sir. Ordinarily, we can trace the sources of these transmissions easily, but this one is elusive. We cannot yet tell who sent it, sir, but it came through the ionosphere. The rabbi said it has the exact same meaning as the message interpreted by their prophet, Daniel, the night before the Babylonian kingdom was taken over by their enemies."

Abilov was angry and shouted, "Why are you bothering me with this? You don't even know who sent it. The meaning must be more cryptic than that, idiot! Do you think I am superstitious? Are we now supposed to listen to a dissident Jew while he dies in prison hating us? Get out of here and come back when you know who sent this message!"

Chapter 40

RECONNAISSANCE

Mt. Whitney, California
November 4
11:30 a.m. (PDT)

Sally and Reggie had been doing their best to gather news by interviewing the military investigators who were, at the same time, trying to interview the two of them. The temperature was getting colder, but they were able to compile and prepare a series of short news articles, as well as a video report using Sally's cell phone camera.

Walking together up the road from their tent, they encountered a man and woman walking toward them. The woman appeared somewhat younger than the man, who was wearing a Forest Service stocking cap and sunglasses but with no other uniform markings.

Sally addressed them together. "Hi, my name is Sally Rogers. This is Reggie Willard. We are with Independence News, reporting on what happened here last night. Can we talk with you for a minute?"

The woman responded, "Hi, my name is Katie. I'm a nurse."

"Hello, Sally. I'm Shane, Forest Service," Alex added.

Katie said, "We are on our way to one of the campsites to help out with some of the children, so we only have a minute or so."

"I understand," Sally said. "Did either of you see what happened last night?"

Katie replied, "Oh no, it was in the middle of the night. I was sound asleep when it happened."

Alex, as Shane said, "I was traveling last night on assignment and had a few mechanical problems I had to deal with. Sorry I can't be of much help."

Reggie asked, "So, when did you arrive here in the canyon?"

Sally raised her phone up and began recording a video of the conversation. When he saw her do this, Shane quickly turned his head and feigned a coughing fit to avoid being recorded.

With that sudden movement, his sunglasses came off. Sally lowered the phone and stepped toward him in an attempt to help.

"Oh, are you okay?" she asked.

As he continued coughing, he bent over, picked up the sunglasses from the pavement, and put them back on. He stood up slowly, and the coughing fit subsided.

"Yeah, thank you," he said. "I think it's the smoke in this canyon. Smells like ash mixed with kerosene."

Reggie joked, "Since you work for the Forest Service, breathing smoke is probably a regular thing for you."

They all laughed politely and went on their way.

Walking along, Sally commented, "Reggie, I'm not so sure about the Forest Service guy. He is handsome, but he's dressed so frumpy. I felt sad when I saw the stocking cap he was wearing too. Remember, it was just like the one Jason Greer was wearing when we visited his cabin. It looks like he didn't make it out before the fire. Can you believe it was only yesterday we spoke with him?"

"No. It's weird. There is so much going on. I can't help wondering if it means something," said Reggie.

"Like what?" asked Sally.

"Like what that pastor was saying about getting things right with God. I didn't know you could do that," Reggie replied.

"My grandmother used to talk about it. She had whatever Shen Kuan has. It's the exact same thing."

***

Though the reporter had gotten only a few seconds of Alex's face on her recording, he knew it could not be a good thing for him.

Katie and Alex walked over to space thirteen, where the church group was. They talked with Larry Gordon for a few minutes. Larry greeted Katie because he recognized her from church. Alex said he was here from the Forest Service, helping to assess what people needed.

Larry addressed Alex and said, "As I'm sure you know, the higher-ups in the Forest Service say we will not be able to leave for probably a few more days. People are getting upset. Aside from the road being obstructed, I think they are looking for a fugitive and want people to stay put, so we are stuck. But we have a question."

"Sure," said Alex.

"How will they help with getting people through the snow after the boulders are cleared from the road? It's not too deep now, but if it storms tonight, it could be a problem."

As if he was speaking on behalf of the Forest Service, Alex said, "That is a good question. I'll check on it. But it should be easy for them, rather, for us, to get a snowplow up here when it's time. What is this about a fugitive?"

"Three people were here about an hour ago asking questions. They said they were with the Forest Service—two men and a woman. I'm a detective, though, and could tell by their questions they are looking for somebody who might be dangerous. Plus, all three of them were carrying the same pistols my special-ops friends like best. Two of them were Glocks with laser sights and the other one was a Beretta 92. I doubt those are Forest Service issue."

Katie asked Larry if he knew of any medical needs she could help with. Larry directed her to Li Jing, who already knew who Katie was and was happy to see her. Li Jing told her that she had seen a guy with a twisted ankle at another campsite who might need some help. She noticed that Katie did not have a first aid kit with her.

Katie said, "I think a bandage or splint will be enough for now."

Li Jing supplied a wrap from her group's first aid kit, and Katie set off to find the guy with the twisted ankle.

He wasn't hard to find. Katie began walking up the narrow road that meandered through the campsite area, and she soon noticed two young men in one of the sites across the road from the group. One had his foot wrapped with a bandage and propped against a metal firepit. The other was attempting to chop wood for a fire.

Their eyes met in a friendly manner, and they all said hello to each other.

Katie said, "I couldn't help noticing your bandage. Were you hurt from the crash?"

"Oh, no," said Nate. "Climbing. It's just a little swollen."

"I'm a nurse. I can look at that bandage if you'd like."

"Okay, thanks," said Nate.

As they talked, both of the friends expressed sadness about the presumed loss of a ranger they admired. Katie dared not mention that she had inside information.

"I'm with the group in site thirteen. I'm sure you guys would be welcome to join the group for dinner," said Katie.

Both were grateful for the invitation and said they would be there.

"Okay. And meanwhile, be sure to pack that ankle in snow.

There's plenty of it."

Katie rejoined Alex after a few more conversations with people in the campground, and they started up the hill toward Jason's ex-home on the way back to the Sidewinder around the crest of the ridge.

Coming closer, they could see that the top of the boulder the cabin had rested on seemed to be sunken in as much as six feet, with broken rock and ash mixed with orange fire retardant over the top. It was as if the giant rock had been hollow and had imploded when the missile hit. It appeared that something might have been inside the rock, but it was impossible to tell what that was. Thirty yards down the driveway from the boulder was a burned-out, upside-down, mangled Jeep. Although it had stopped burning, thin, wispy clouds of black smoke were still rising from the three smoldering tires that remained.

A guard was standing on the grounds. However, Alex and Katie were able to hike on by, unnoticed, because he was looking out toward the cloud-covered valley and, ironically, smoking a cigarette.

Finally, they arrived at the snowmobile and began waiting for Jeanie. It was cold. Instinctively, they embraced each other to share the heat.

Alex said, "Okay, this is a smart idea. It is so cold out here."

"Yes, 'smart'," she said with a wry tone.

Pulling her even closer, Alex said, "You seem to be the only source of warmth on this mountain."

"I was just thinking the same thing about you," she said.

"I'm not exactly warm. In fact, I thought I would probably freeze to death," he said.

"You mean last night when you went swimming in the lake?"

"No, always—until just now."

"Just now?" she said.

"Yes, just now," he said.

"We're not talking about the weather, are we?"

"I guess not."

After a few moments of silence, he asked, "Have you ever met somebody for the first time, but you feel like you already know them?"

"Only just now," she said.

"Same here," he said.

A few pleasant minutes later, they heard Jeanie's voice: "You two look warm and cozy! Let's go before we all freeze solid."

Jeanie had been walking in the cold for quite a while. In her knapsack was food she bought while she was doing reconnaissance at the little store. She had also confirmed what they all suspected: that this was more of a manhunt than a plane crash investigation. Greg the manager at the store, noticed it. He told her that "two heavily armed rangers" had been there asking him questions. He said, "Ranger uniforms are becoming a popular disguise lately."

Jeanie climbed onto the Sidewinder with Katie and Alex. Alex started the engine, and they rumbled off.

Periodically, they stopped to sweep snow over parts of the tracks made by the snowmobile. Whenever the terrain would allow, they got away from the trail as an attempt to be less conspicuous. One more snowfall and it would not be a problem, but since they were being hunted by professionals, they did not want to leave clues. Because of this extra work, it took longer to get back to the hut. When they arrived, they hid the Sidewinder in the same bush as before, then camouflaged it again, this time more thoroughly, and began walking toward the shelter. As they got closer, Alex signaled the two women to veer left toward a group of trees, took out his handgun, and approached the building from the side, away from the door. He knocked on the corner brace, then heard Jason's voice behind him.

"You're back!" He had come out from behind a tree. "I've been watching you from over there."

Alex had quickly raised his gun, ready to engage an enemy; then, realizing who it was, he lowered it to his side. "Not a good idea to sneak up on me," he said sharply. "I'm glad it's you, though. How are things here?"

"No visitors or problems. I covered up the hut more with branches and snow. The next snowfall will practically seal it up."

They all went inside and warmed up near the stove while Jason prepared dinner for the others, thanks to Jeanie's foresight in bringing back food.

As they were eating, Katie reported what they had learned to Jason. "We found out there is a manhunt going on. At least three armed agents were snooping around the camp area and Jeanie learned they had been to the store at the end of the road.

"Agents are posing as Forest Service people. No one can leave the area, partly because the road is blocked by a piece of Alex's plane, along with a big pile of boulders it knocked off the cliff. Now there are a bunch of campers and some cabin people who are stuck there until further notice. We saw Forest Service workers beginning to supply food for people, so it may be a few more days."

Jeanie said, "Should we just wait here until the search is off?"

"If we wait too long, they will end up here," Alex replied.

Katie said, "At the campground, I ran into someone Jeanie and I both know. Jeanie knows her better than I do. It's the pastor's wife from our church. They are camping there as a group."

Suddenly a light came on for Jeanie: "Li Jing, of course! This is their last camping trip of the season. If we assimilate with them, we could leave when they do. I could say I came to the canyon looking for my brother, which is true. Katie is also a member of the congregation and, since she is a nurse, she can keep helping people through this crisis. If they are willing, Alex could lay low with the group until we are all able to leave together. After we are out of the canyon, and Alex is taking his next step, Jason could show up alive. We could say that Alex and Katie are—"

Katie wittingly turned to Alex: "Colonel Larson, would you like to be my boyfriend?"

The man who made the extreme decision to eject from a fighter jet in a nanosecond was paralyzed by the possible dual meaning of that invitation. Then, coming to his senses, he said, "Your boyfriend? Damn right I would."

They all laughed.

Jason was quiet, thinking. Then, he said, "That might work, but I don't like how this plan could incriminate those people."

Alex said, "He's right."

Jeanie said, "It would be their decision. They could say no, and we would find another solution."

Alex said, "You could say I made you do it at gunpoint."

"Opposed," said Katie, Jeanie, and Jason in turn.

"We're voting now?" Alex asked.

Jason said, "We haven't enlisted yet, sir."

"All right then," said Alex, "we'll go back tomorrow early after some rest. Jeanie and Katie, are you up for another cold ride?"

Both of them nodded.

"Okay, we sleep next, then eat and go," he said.

In the shelter, there were only three cots. About mid-summer, there had been four, but one of them was needed for a fire operation on the other side of Mt. Whitney. While Jason and the two women were talking, Alex took a couple of blankets and one of the sleeping bags from the bin in the corner, laid the blankets out on the floor, and got into the bag. In less than a minute, and before anyone could make a courtesy offer for him to use one of the cots. he was asleep.

Chapter 41

PRESUMED DEAD

Bishop, California
November 4
6:00 p.m. (PDT)

News anchor Rose McPherson was beginning the evening news report.

"Good evening. Tonight, we have General Clarence Peterson of the United States Air Force to comment on the incident in the mountains above the town of Lone Pine. General, thank you for coming on with us tonight."

"Certainly," said General Peterson.

"We have various accounts of what happened last night on Mt. Whitney. Can you clarify this for us?" said Rose.

"Yes, Rose. As I'm sure you know, war leaves its mark on everyone, especially those who are directly involved in combat situations. They may come back with no discernable symptoms of Post-Traumatic Stress Disorder until they are suddenly triggered into a state of fear or even a flashback. I hate to say that, in this case, one of our pilots, Lieutenant Colonel Alex Larson, seems to have experienced one of these triggers while he was delivering two specialized weapons to Edwards Air Force Base. He suddenly diverted from his flight plan, flew into the canyon, and fired one of the missiles randomly into a structure on a hillside—a cabin. Then he crashed the plane into a cliff further up the canyon, quite possibly when he realized what he had done."

"And Colonel Larson?" asked Rose.

"Regrettably, he was killed in the crash," said Peterson.

"This is sobering. Reports we have say that the cabin was owned by a man who works as a ranger for the Forest Service, Jason Greer, but it has not been confirmed if he was at home at the time of the blast."

"Well, Rose, I can say that unless he shows up, it's unlikely to be confirmed because of the type of weapon that was fired. There will be nothing left to find. We can only hope he turns up soon."

Rose concluded, "Thank you, General. That's it so far. We'll have to wait for more developments in this story. No doubt we will be having future discussions about how PTSD is affecting our servicemen and women."

Chapter 42

OPEN SEASON

Mammoth Ski Resort, California
November 4
4:30 p.m. (PDT)

Yerik Orlov heard the notification on his phone. For the moment he ignored it because he was at a bank flirting with the teller. Each Friday, he deposited his earnings from his job at the Ghost Pine Restaurant, where he was a waiter part-time. Orlov was outgoing and good at his job. People enjoyed his sense of humor, great service, and unusual accent.

In the small ski resort of Mammoth, near the town of Bishop, there were not many people from Kazakhstan. People found it interesting to listen, and banter with him. Mammoth was also an unlikely place to find an undercover agent from the Russian Federal Security Service. He had been at the resort for the last eight months, getting to know certain tourists who were influential in government or business, romancing some of the women when he could, and gleaning valuable information for his government's interest. He was especially good at harvesting inside information about the next financial moves with governments and big tech companies. While he never picked anyone's literal pocket, a lot of people who thought their valuable stories and inside information were safe with Orlov were sadly mistaken.

Orlov had other talents. He had received special training from the Russians when he lived in Moscow for a few years. From there he had been given numerous assignments, some of which involved assassination. Even though he enjoyed the pleasures of living in a ski resort in America, the intrigue of his covert job, and the women, who were always available and looking for adventure—despite all these things, he was getting restless for another assignment.

After work, he checked his messages on a special phone app equipped with PGP encryption. The message included a link to a video news report featuring a man in a Forest Service stocking cap. He appeared to be reaching for a pair of sunglasses falling from his face. Along with the video link was an enhanced frame—a clear picture of the man's face. The accompanying message was made up of short statements: "Follow this news story. Apply your talents with this man immediately. Confirm completion. Last sighted at Whitney Portal area. On the run. Armed. Begin search near Consultation and Meysan Lakes from John Muir Trail. Kash will have a snowmobile ready for you at 0600, Mammoth Ski Shop."

Orlov smiled. *I will sleep well tonight,* he thought. *Tomorrow, we hunt.*

Chapter 43

HOPING FOR ALLIES

Mt. Whitney, California
November 5
8:00 a.m. (PDT)

At the shelter, the night passed quietly. No explosions, sirens, crashes, gunshots, or bear horns. Alex opened his eyes with a start. There was such a stark difference between sleeping peacefully and running for one's life that he had to take a minute to adjust. Across the room, Katie was lying on a cot, asleep. Jason and his sister were awake, sitting at the table in the kitchen area, playing cards. Alex could smell coffee.

Alex felt comfortable until he tried to move. That's when he became aware of every muscle in his body. His knee and his arm were sore from being bashed and twisted on his way down to earth the night before last. Pushing the pain aside, he sat up, then eventually stood.

Alex walked over and sat down on the cot that was parallel to Katie's and looked at her. She was still sleeping. He was fascinated by how peaceful she looked. Her eyes opened and met his.

"Good morning," he said.

Jeanie, with her back to him and not realizing he was addressing Katie, said, "Good morning."

Katie smiled and said it back to Alex and then to Jason and Jeanie. They all repeated it jokingly. Then she said it again in a softer, private tone to Alex, who was still looking at her. He smiled.

Despite his fondness for Pop-Tarts, Jason liked to cook real food for people when he had the opportunity. He began looking through the cabinet for food he could use to prepare breakfast for his guests.

While they were eating, they reviewed their plans. Alex, Katie, and Jeanie would go to the campground together. Jeanie would check out the possibility of assimilating with Shen Kuan's group and leaving with them as they drove to Independence when the road was cleared. Meanwhile, Alex had been formulating his plan to further his escape after leaving the mountain.

After a late breakfast, they were ready to leave for the campground. Alex had stuffed some extra clothes, including socks and another jacket, plus everything from his survival kit, into a green and white backpack that was in the hut as a replacement for his military pack.

Standing outside the shelter, the three said their goodbyes to Jason who, according to the plan, would stay for a couple more days before he made his appearance.

All four gathered outside.

Alex, offering his hand to Jason, said, "I'm glad we met. Thanks for keeping me from freezing to death."

"Thanks for blowing up my house," said Jason with a wry smile.

"Any time," Alex replied.

Then Jason asked, "By the way, did you and Katie see a green Jeep at the cabin site yesterday?"

Alex asked, "How many wheels?"

"Four. You know, four-wheel drive."

Alex tried his best to keep a straight face but nearly lost it. Shaking her head, Katie answered for him. "No, not four wheels." Glancing at Alex, then back, she added, "Green? Nope."

It was time to go. Jeanie and Jason hugged. Then Alex, Jeanie, and Katie set out toward where the Sidewinder was hidden.

Looking over his shoulder, Alex yelled, "Remember, shoot back."

In a few minutes, they were underway. It was getting colder. The cloud cover was thickening.

Chapter 44

HATE BUT HELP THINE ENEMY

Almaty, Kazakhstan
November 5
10:00 p.m. (ALMT)
14 Hours Ahead of California

Tamir Abilov was at his desk, feeling anxious, waiting on word from a ski resort in California, USA. Occasionally, and secretly, Abilov had wished to visit the United States. The prosperity, the ingenuity, and the freedom had appealed to him. But he had to admit that a visit there was out of the question. Such freedom, he believed, made prosperity and ingenuity too dangerous for the common person.

Today, the message he was waiting for was much more important than any of that. Yerik Orlov, the assassin, was now his best hope for unlocking the weapon and for obtaining a status report on the situation in the United States.

Aside from Stephan Benetti, other intelligence sources had

provided him with information. He was aware that the small band of Americans were as intent on unlocking the weapon as he was and that they had a better fix on the DNA targets. Many events of the last few days had been brought to his attention, and from these he could infer from a distance what the targets were.

Abilov's hatred for Americans was almost matched by his respect for their military rigor and attention to safety. He knew it was not a stupid accident that this fighter jet fired on a vacation home in the Sierra Mountains, or that one of its missiles just happened to detonate onboard the plane. Too many countermeasures are built into American military equipment for that to occur.

Obviously, the incident was a botched attempt on the pilot's life—botched, he knew, because what Abilov called the "Voodoo weapon" had not yet worked. He knew this because he and his accomplices were still alive. There was still time to strike first after letting the Americans do most of the work.

Nazarov had informed Abilov about Sundheim's son—that he was the known source of DNA keeping the weapon locked. And now, they had a picture of him, clipped from Sally Rogers' montage video.

Rasul Musin knocked briefly, then entered the room.

"Has there been any word?" he asked.

"Not yet," Abilov replied.

"Timing is important," said Rasul.

"Timing is everything. If Orlov kills the pilot, we can depend on the Americans to ensure that the DNA is destroyed by cremating the body."

Rasul said, "No doubt, they will do it as quickly as they can too."

Abilov was sure his comrade was correct. Certainly, the Americans would take care of this task, and quickly, because they knew both sides were after the same thing—namely, each other. At the very moment the pilot's body would be cremated, the quick-draw contest between the ambitious contingent at Almaty and the one at China Lake would begin.

"We need to know exactly when that moment arrives," said Abilov.

Finally, the message from Orlov came in by text. He had responded from Mammoth, California to his new assignment with a short answer in Russian: "Уезжаю прямо сейчас"—"I am leaving right now."

Chapter 45

ANOTHER FAILING GRADE

China Lake, California
November 5
10:00 a.m. (PDT)

So much time was spent in either Bundy's or Connor's offices in a twenty-four-hour period that the generals and colonel could have moved in for convenience. What was originally an attempt to keep an enemy from acquiring ultimate power was turning into a major damage control and clean-up project. The longer it took, the more likely it was for the other side to get control of the weapon first. At a time when secrecy was essential, the specter of an aerial strike by a fighter jet had undoubtedly tipped off the other side, as well as the rest of the world, to look in this direction. The China Lake group could only hope that their target, Alex Larson, was unknown to the Almaty group.

At China Lake, the team did not know for certain how far along Abilov and his cohorts had gotten in their quest to find the right DNA source and unlock the weapon. The indicator for who unlocked it first would be who died first. Thus, the need to enable the weapon as quickly as possible became the justification for neglecting an important piece of the puzzle—there was still no real plan for locking the weapon after it was used.

Colonel Olson had just arrived with new intelligence. A message had been picked up early that morning and delivered to him. Oddly, it did not seem to be heavily encrypted.

"Gentlemen, this is a ULF message picked up this morning. Because of our submarine communication breach, I told our team to apprise me of any transmissions that are questionable. This one may or may not be related, but it is very unsettling because it seems to defy our normal ability to find the source. Recently, we tracked a couple of tech students who made a ULF device for entertainment and were transmitting idiotic messages into the ionosphere. They were creating havoc, so at first, we thought it may have come from them. However, we confirmed that their equipment was confiscated before this message came in. Now, bottom line, we can't tell where it came from.

"Arabic is the language of the message, and it mimics a biblical text: 'Mene, mene, tekel.'"

Upon hearing this, Connor suddenly felt nauseated. Certain items from his conscience, which he had effectively stifled until now, came close to the surface. He was familiar with the "writing on the wall" story. According to the story, that message came from God in the form of a hand which was seen writing it on a wall during a wild party in the palace of a king. In a drunken state, the king of Babylon had publicly mocked God's rightful standing by using gold cups from the Jewish temple worship to serve up more wine for his party guests. That night, the great empire of Babylon was turned over to the Persian army. At that time, it was a message of impending judgement toward Babylon.

"It sounds like another amateur scientist," Connor said, "interfering with serious intelligence gathering."

Bundy asked, "Does it fit into any other class of messaging you have seen before?"

"No, sir," said Olsen.

"How about the Arabic part? Sounds like it fits more with the Middle Eastern operations," said Morrison.

Olsen replied, "Possibly, but it was reviewed for that before it came to me."

"Unless you find any other way this could be relevant, dump it. We have more critical things to worry about. But tell them to keep working on tracking the source and to put a stop to it," said Bundy.

Connor agreed—outwardly. Inwardly, he felt uneasy.

<u>Chapter 46</u>

A TICKET OUT OF HERE

Mt. Whitney, California
November 5
11:00 a.m. (PDT)

On the way back to the campground, Alex, Katie, and Jeanie stopped numerous times to cover their tracks. Arriving at the same place over the ridge as they had the day before, they hid the Sidewinder and hiked into the Portal area. Once again going in different directions, Jeanie headed directly to space thirteen, hoping to find Li Jing and Shen Kuan to see if they would consider helping with their plan. Alex and Katie went a different direction, gathering information, and would circle back toward the campsite to hear the verdict from Jeanie.

Alex and Katie decided to divert their path to the trail beside the creek to minimize their visible presence, then head up to the road again. Snow on the ground made the trail slippery, but they steadied each other. Alex had something on his mind.

"Hey, about yesterday afternoon," he said.

Katie laughed. "You mean when we were romantic on the back of a snowmobile?" She laughed again, enjoying his awkwardness.

"You have to admit we were freezing, so we needed to get warm," he said.

"You have to admit that it was kind of nice," she replied.

"Yes. I do," admitted Alex.

They continued walking to where the trail joined the road again. Up ahead, about fifty feet, Alex saw a man and woman with Forest Service patches on their green jackets walking toward them. He noticed they were each carrying a pistol on their hip—his on the left, hers on the right. Quickly, Alex turned away from them and pulled Katie to himself. As he embraced her, he said in her ear, "Pretend to kiss me, right now."

She did. And he did. His left hand was at the small of her back. His right was on the knurled handle of the weapon on his hip covered by his jacket. They kept at it long enough for the two agents to pass by. After that, they were not pretending anymore, and during those few moments they stepped away from the relentless threats and problems that filled their world. It was like a gift. Reluctantly, they came out of it and began walking again.

"About just now," Alex joked.

They both laughed.

Alex said, "You realize this may not last. They are trying to kill me."

Katie replied, "But you're not dead yet. Whatever happens, Alex, this is way bigger than both of us."

"I agree," he said.

They started walking in the direction of space thirteen. Jeanie was coming toward them, smiling.

She said, "Lunch is in a few minutes. Dinner is at six. We each have a tent ready. Alex will be with Larry Gordon. Shen and Li Jing understand what is happening and they are all in. Shen says the bad news is that he hears Larry snoring two tents away. We can lay low with the group until the road is clear and people are allowed to leave. Then we ride back to town in different vehicles."

Alex said, "That works, but I need to take care of something first."

Jeanie asked, "What do you have in mind?"

"It will be best if I'm not in this campground for a while. There is a lot of official activity, plus the snowmobile is parked too close and they may be looking for it by now. I'm going to run some food back to Jason, change into different clothes, then come back here when it gets darker. I'll hide the snowmobile better and further away. You two should be safe because you are already part of the group here."

Katie said, "I don't like this plan. Why don't you just stay in the tent and wait things out?"

"I will later, but this will help keep things low-key, which is what we need. I'll be back after dark," Alex replied.

"You are a stubborn man," said Katie.

Alex took off his sunglasses to clean them. Katie and Alex exchanged a glance before he put the sunglasses back on and walked up the road toward the ridge.

Jeanie noticed the exchange—nothing escaped her awareness. "What was that?"

"Just something," said Katie.

Just then, Li Jing approached and offered to show them their accommodations.

<u>Chapter 47</u>

SUBJECT SPOTTED

Mt. Whitney, California
November 5
12:00 p.m. (PDT)

Outside the store at the upper end of Mt. Whitney Portal Road stood a man reading a text on his phone. He was one of the three special agents tasked with finding and eliminating a certain missing pilot. Included in the text was a single frame from Sally Rogers' video report to the news agency. Taken the moment Alex's sunglasses had fallen off, the frame provided a clear view of his face.

The text read, "Target I.D., Lt. Colonel Alex Larson. Incognito, possibly blending in with Forest Service personnel."

Moments later, the two other agents, who were in the campground area further down the road, received his forwarded text warning them to watch for that person of interest.

One of the agents, Lauren Haines, remembered seeing someone matching the description heading up a steep hill toward the ridge. She turned back in that direction.

***

Alex made it to the snowmobile and pulled off the branches and the snow they had put on it a few hours earlier. Ignition key in hand, he swung his leg over the seat and started the engine. Not much warm-up was needed. As the Sidewinder began to accelerate, he glanced back and to his left, and noticed a woman in a Forest Service uniform yelling something at him. Though he could not hear her words over the roar of the engine, he was certainly not stopping. A moment later, he saw her bend her knees, raise her gun, and point it at him. Alex ducked his head and turned the throttle up all the way, letting the Sidewinder do what it was designed for.

Unfortunately, it was not designed to outrun a bullet. He heard a sharp clank, then another one. A third projectile pierced his backpack and was deflected by the blade of the big knife inside. Another bullet just missed his shoulder and hit a pine tree ahead of him. A piece of bark, dislodged by the impact of the lead, flew off and hit him in the temple as he drove into its path. He didn't notice where the other bullets landed, but he looked back in time to see the agent shoving a fresh clip into her gun. She was serious.

"Damn, she is way too good," he said out loud.

Alex knew he dared not give her another opportunity to fire. He had to put more distance between them. Normally, pistols are best for short range; however, he could tell this agent's skill was beyond normal. She was about to shoot again when he veered to the right, hoping to lose her in the trees. To throw her off, he wanted her to see his new direction, knowing that she would tell her fellow agents and they would try to intercept him.

After going a little further, he came to an area with no snow on the ground after a small rockslide. There, he made a sharp turn in the other direction—toward the lake, a change of course that the agent would not have seen.

Alex knew that his trackers would be looking for a big, loud snowmobile that they could easily follow. He had to get rid of it.

Since he had eluded them for now, his situation was starting to look slightly better—that is until he smelled gasoline. One of that sharpshooter agent's bullets had punctured the gas tank and it was leaking. A quick inspection revealed that the hole was low enough to leak out most of the gasoline. The motor was still running, though, so he continued with a plan he had begun to formulate just after the shooting started.

At the rate he was traveling, Alex was about six minutes from Meysan Lake, provided he could keep up his pace. Working his way through the trees and over occasionally exposed rocks was tricky and slowed him down because the snow was not very deep. Finally, he saw the lake about a hundred yards ahead.

At fifty yards from the eastern shore, he diverted the vehicle into the middle of a small group of pine trees and stopped, letting the engine idle. As quickly as he could, he took off his backpack and threw it on the ground in the snow, along with his jacket, shirt, gloves, socks, and shoes, then tossed them on top of the pack. Next came his belt with the gun in the holster, his pants, and his green stocking cap. Feeling a tinge of modesty, he left his skivvies on. As he stood there, nearly naked in the forest with snow all around, never would he have been mistaken for a person in his right mind.

As Alex got back on the ice-cold Sidewinder, he felt the sting of the cold plastic seat and the frigid air. "I hate cold water!" he said out loud.

As he took one deep breath, contemplating what he was about to do, he reminded himself that there was no other choice. Then, letting out an exasperated sigh, he said quietly, "Shit."

Alex revved the engine all the way, engaging the clutch, and the machine sped off, directly toward the lake.

Snowmobiles are heavy, as much as six hundred pounds, and they do not float. However, they will skim across the surface of the water if they are moving fast enough, and this one was fast. Alex reached the shore at well over sixty miles per hour and shot out onto the lake. As the Sidewinder hit the water, it was immediately enveloped with spray kicked up by the front skis and treads and appeared to be sinking. However, it continued to lunge forward through the canopy of spray and skimmed across the water. Once he was well into the lake, about forty yards, he drew his thumb across the red kill button to stop the engine, but before he could push it, the thunderous machine stopped on its own—out of gas. Keven Bales' new Sidewinder snowmobile slowed and quickly sank into the icy water. Steam, bubbles, and a tortured crackling noise floated up as six hundred pounds of hot metal sank down into the lake.

Alex tried to anticipate the nearly freezing temperature of the water, but it did little to mitigate the sudden painful shock wave as his body became fully immersed. His lungs refused to function until, slowly and deliberately, he forced himself to breathe. Most of his physical distress began to subside as his skin became numb. However, he realized how quickly heat was leaving his body.

With that realization, two other crystal-clear thoughts came to him: first, *There is a lot of expensive junk at the bottom of this lake.* The next, he said out loud in a quivering voice: "I have to get out of this damn ice water!"

Swimming as hard as he could warmed him slightly and got him close enough to the shore for his bare feet to touch the sharp, granite-gravel bottom. Alex, trudging up the incline of this miniature beach and out of the water might have made a good beer commercial in sunny, warm Mexico. Unfortunately, there was no beer. Instead, once again, he was freezing and running for his life.

He ran up the beach and across the snow in his bare feet and wet skivvies to where he had left his clothes and gear, then dried himself off with one of the T-shirts he had put in his backpack.

Although going for a swim was not what he had in mind at the shelter when he had stuffed the backpack, it contained just what he needed now—a few extra layers of clothes. Even more than lucky was the discovery that the clothes he got from Jason's cardboard box included a pair of long underwear, a valuable piece of mountain gear. Alex hated long underwear, but not as much as he hated cold water. And in his situation, they were far better than sopping wet, icy, short underwear and lessened the danger of hypothermia. So, at the risk of appearing even more deranged than he did already—standing there naked in the forest—he made the swap.

When Alex was fully dressed in as many layers as possible, he felt his body slowly warming up again. He took the other garments he was not wearing and put them in the pack rather than leaving them there to be discovered by trackers.

No longer could he go back to the shelter because of the possibility that the three agents would be working their way toward that area.

Too bad, he thought. *It would have been a shorter hike than going back to the Portal Campground, but it's not worth the risk.*

Losing the agents had cost him, because now he was on foot. However, it was to his advantage that his pursuers would be looking for him, and the snowmobile, in another direction. With the agents busy at the upper end of the canyon, he hoped to be able to hike back to the campground and arrive sometime after dark. At that point, he could slip into the tent they had ready for him and lay low until he could leave with the group, possibly the next day.

Alex began the long trek back.

Chapter 48

MAN DOWN

Mt. Whitney, California
November 5
5:15 p.m. (PDT)

Snow clouds still hung low over the canyon. Alex heard the muffled crunch of snow with each step. Except in places where he could see clearly, he stayed mostly off the trail. He did not want his pursuers to get a clear view of him—or a clear shot.

Ahead of him was the remainder of what he knew was one very long walk in the cold. In about an hour, it would be dark except for moonlight. He knew the way to the campground from his recent treks up and down the ridge, but he could only estimate how long it would take on foot. Two or three hours seemed reasonable at this intermittent rate. Alex was still not very far from the shelter and too close to where he had re-directed the agents, so he had to get away from there. Making it back to the campground in this roundabout way was tough, but a much more welcome challenge than having to outrun trained killers who knew where he was.

"It's a good thing no one knows where the Sidewinder really is,"

Alex mumbled to himself.

Along the trail to his right was a drop-off in most places. On the other side, the hill ascended in a steep but more even way, forming higher ground. Alex was making good time, moving along a stretch of the trail with a slightly downward slope when he noticed that his right shoelace was untied. After pulling off his gloves and stuffing them in his jacket pocket, he stopped walking and stooped down to retie the lace. However, the sound of his footsteps continued for two more steps before stopping. It was as if a ghost version of himself had kept walking and making that soft crunch sound in the snow. A ghost? No—above and slightly behind him to the left, where the sound came from, he saw the figure of a man in the fading light. Uncannily, the man was wearing a dark blue jacket and a green stocking cap, like his own. It was the second time today he saw a stranger pointing a gun at him.

Alex spun around, still in a crouched position, and began running back up the trail toward a big pine tree standing alongside it. Before he got to the tree, his own gun was out and pointed up the hill.

The visitor, Yerik Orlov, changed position to reacquire his target at the new location.

Adrenaline is an invaluable resource when it is time to fight, and Orlov was not the only one trained in combat. Alex's call sign, "Savage One," was an accurate reflection of his instinct for concentrated aggression in battle. As a pilot, his battle experience was in the air with a different weapon than Orlov's; yet, when the need of the moment was violence, he did not hesitate.

Each man was a mirror image of the other. Alex's left hand came up to join his right on the pistol grip. He brought the pale green dot of his front sight to rest between the two on the back of the gun slide and squarely onto Orlov's neck, his finger tightening on the trigger. Suddenly, Orlov's arms flew up as if he was going to shoot at something in the sky. Blood exploded from the man's forehead and sprayed the white snow in front of him red. The sound of three more shots rang out from behind the man, muted by some distance and the acoustic softening of the snow. Orlov's blue jacket was suddenly spotted with three darker-red blotches, visible on both front and back as his body twisted all the way around and fell headfirst down the hill.

Alex had not fired his gun. Whoever had certainly did him a favor, but there was no wasting time to find out or thank anybody. He could only rely on the possibility that he had not been seen.

Voices came from further up the hill, above where the shots had hit their mark, and became louder as they confirmed their accomplishment with each other. By then, Alex was out of sight and moving as fast as he could over the snowy terrain, sliding downward from the trail and struggling to move parallel with it at the same time.

***

All three agents appeared over the crest of the hill, out of breath.

"I would hate to be in your sights, Haines," said Aaron, one of the agents.

Lance, the agent next to him, chimed in, "Yeah, don't ever get her mad."

Lauren Haines was trembling from her own adrenaline and from facing the hard reality that they had just killed a man. She valued her conscience and took no personal pleasure in the assignment.

"Thanks, but it looks like we all hit him. This is Larson; same green hat, blue jacket, carrying a pistol, on the run."

"Not much left of his face though," said Lance.

"Right. Let's get the chopper in here. Send the coordinates," Aaron said. "They want the body and all traces just as soon as we nab him. This guy must have been into some deep shit."

"I would say so—he went rogue and blew up a cabin with somebody in it, started a forest fire, and crashed a fighter jet into a cliff," said Lance.

Haines replied, "That would be enough to piss off his bosses for a 'shoot to kill.' It's never easy, though."

"It's a good thing we spotted his stolen snowmobile," commented Aaron. "Why do you think he left it on the trail like that?"

Lance answered, "I don't know—maybe for the same reason he snapped and fired those missiles."

"Maybe. Well, we got him. That's what they wanted," said Lauren.

***

All four officers were present in General Bundy's office, as they had been for many hours, waiting for news from the manhunt.

Olsen hung up after finishing a phone call.

"They got him. Four shots, one to the head." Olsen felt slightly nauseated.

"Is this a confirmed kill?" asked Bundy.

"On the ground, yes," said Olsen. "Everything matched the description, including his clothes. He was also armed and on the run. His face was unrecognizable, but otherwise, it all fits. A chopper is on the way to retrieve the body."

Bundy said, "Call them back. Tell them to collect every bit of blood and tissue. Then to get everything cremated as soon as possible. When that is done, I want immediate confirmation. If anyone has a problem with that, tell them the order comes from me."

Chapter 49

TO DREAM?

Mt. Whitney, California
November 5
5:15 p.m. (PDT)

Around five o'clock, another military helicopter flew very fast over the campground, toward the end of the canyon, and over the ridge in the direction of Meysan Lake. It was low and loud enough that the branches of the tallest pine trees shook and swayed violently as if they were angry. A while later, the same chopper came back, just as fast, this time traveling more in the direction of China Lake.

Katie was standing directly under the chopper when it flew over the first time. She felt the irresistible force from the rotors and wind, which violently disturbed everything that was not tied down. For her, it was like being drenched in sheer powerlessness. Everything she wished she could control was out of her hands. Still, she retained a kind of hopeful expectation—faith perhaps?—that Alex would survive. When the aircraft flew over the second time, she was alarmed but not beaten.

Jeanie and Katie were keeping a low profile, assisting in the camp with dinner, and feeling grateful to the Kuans for helping them. Li

Jing came over to where they were working and said, "The Forest Service brought some heavy equipment up from the town of Bishop to try to clear the road, and they have been 'working' on it all day. Shen is suspicious, though, because they only brought one backhoe and a dump truck rather than enough equipment to clear the rocks and wreckage in a much shorter time."

Jeanie said, "Sounds to me like an orchestrated lack of equipment to slow the whole thing down so they can find the person they are looking for."

"Yes," said Katie.

At about six o'clock, dinner was ready. More people from the larger camp area had joined in. Although everyone was tired, there was a feeling of solidarity because of their common predicament. Most brought food to share, and morale was good.

Sally and Reggie were becoming regulars with an open meal invitation. Both felt welcome and relaxed. Logan and Sheri were there too and, as it had been from the start, both Sally and Reggie found it especially easy to talk with them. Sadie's mother, Finnie, was there also, as well as Gina's mother, Jessie.

Sitting across from Shen, Larry noticed his eyes looking tired and commented, "You thought we were only going for one last campout before winter. A lot has happened in the last few days."

Shen snickered, "We did not expect a plane crash or being trapped in the mountains."

Logan said to Larry, "I've been thinking. The other night, what if that missile had gone off-course, or what if that big piece of fighter jet lying on the road over there had come down just eighty yards in our direction, on top of us—let's say on top of your tent, Larry? You would be dead."

"Yes, unless I was wearing my Iron Man suit," Larry said playfully.

Logan laughed, "True. But if you didn't have your suit on—let's say you forgot it—and you died, what then?"

Larry said, "I can say there was a time the thought of dying used to scare the hell out of me. Not getting hit by airplane parts—but death. I did my best not to think about it, but it kept coming back to haunt me like a ghost in an old house."

Reggie said, "I used to worry about that too, but I don't anymore."

"Why not?" said Larry.

"First," he said, "I got pretty good at distracting myself from thinking about it. Later, though, I concluded that all I am is a hell of a lot of chemical reactions bundled up together, so when I die, it's all over. That's it. I finally gave up expecting anything more than that. Now, I live for what I like to do, have some relationships, and work. I don't worry about it, aside from an occasional philosophical moment after a couple shots of brandy."

"How do you handle that?" said Larry.

"A little more brandy settles it," joked Reggie.

Everyone laughed.

Logan said, "When I was younger, there was a time when I was in serious despair because I lost someone I was in love with. I was thinking about killing myself, but I had second thoughts."

Shen said, "Like Hamlet?"

"Exactly," said Logan. "Wait, I thought you were from China. What do they know about Hamlet?"

He laughed, "I do read English, Logan."

Larry asked, "I have heard of Hamlet, but who actually is he?"

Logan answered, "Hamlet is a character in a play by that name. Shakespeare wrote it. In the play, Hamlet is the Prince of Denmark."

Finnie said, "I was supposed to read that in college, but instead, I was getting high in my dorm room when the assignment was due."

Logan continued, "Well, in the play, this guy Hamlet thinks a lot, and he is thinking himself into a very dark place, to the point that he is considering suicide. He had reason to be troubled because his father had recently died, then right away, his mother married his uncle, who took over the throne. Well, late one night, Hamlet is up on the castle wall, brooding about all this, and he sees the ghost of his father. The ghost tells him something like, 'Your uncle killed me so he could marry your mother and be king. Now I want you to avenge my death by killing your uncle.'"

Finnie said, "That is so cringey! What does he do?"

"For a long time, he is indecisive, not trusting his own perception. One day, while he is sinking in morbid thoughts, he walks through the cemetery and gets into a conversation with the grave digger. They happen to find the skull of the guy who used to take care of Hamlet when he was a young boy. His name was Yorick and, of course, he was dead."

"Of course," said Sheri wittily.

"So, the thought of Yorick being dead makes Hamlet even more hopeless, and that is when he says the famous—"

"Oh, I know this!" Reggie stood up with an actor's persona and quoted forcefully from the play, "'To be or not to be. That is the question'. . ."

Embarrassed at first, Sally covered her face with her hands, then laughed along with everyone as he kept reciting the lines: "'Whether 'tis nobler in the mind to suffer the slings and arrows of outrageous fortune, or to take arms against a sea of troubles, and by opposing, end them? To die: to sleep . . . sleep: perchance to dream: ay, there's the rub; for in that sleep of death what dreams may come. . .'"

With cheers and laughter, everyone at the table applauded. The other people in the camp looked on with amusement.

Shen joked, "This is proof that you went to class that day, unlike Finnie."

"So, anyway," Logan continued, "I was in the same dark place as Hamlet, thinking that dying might be like sleeping. Then, also like Hamlet, I realized there is probably something after that, like dreaming when you are asleep. But then, it would be too late to do anything about it. Later, I became convinced that there is a whole lot more beyond this life."

Li Jing commented, "I think most people have felt despair like this. At the worst time of my life, I have. But a friend asked me, 'What if dying puts us in the presence of God? What if God and Christ are really true?'"

"Then I would be screwed," said Finnie.

"Me too," said Jessie with a slightly cynical giggle.

Reggie turned to Shen and asked, "Shen, mind if I ask you a question?"

"Sure."

"You and Li Jing obviously believe in God and Christ and all that. With everything you have been through—you know, jail and losing your freedom and all the rest—what makes you still believe that it's all true?"

"Definitely I do not want to believe something without a good reason, or because somebody says I should. I first learned about it through a friend at the university in Beijing. I thought he was being naïve because all I knew about the Bible came from people who were making fun of it. But I was intrigued because I respected him, and he was certainly not a gullible person. He invited me to study it with him and see for myself what it said. So, for about a year, I brought all my challenges and questions, and we studied it together. During that time, my confidence in it grew because it made sense and I saw how reliable it is.

"Later that year, I went through a terrible time of emotional pain and turmoil when my hopes for the career I had been working for were dissolving. In my distress, I prayed to Jesus the way it is described in the Bible and asked for help. Right then, I was given a deep peace I had never known before—an assurance that God was real, and that I was not abandoned."

"Looks like most of it, for you, comes from personal experience then," said Sally.

"A big part of it—but then I started looking into the prophecies of the Bible and found that they give certainty to many of the teachings by predicting historic events and people. For instance, this is how we can identify Jesus as the Christ."

Logan added, "I'm familiar with some of those prophecies. They shed light on a lot of the trouble we are having in the world, even today. Personally, I welcome this because I still say—even when it's not spiritual, there is usually a lot more going on backstage than we get to see."

Reggie added, "Right—like, why would a highly-trained pilot 'accidentally' fire a live missile at a random cabin in the woods?"

Shen added, "Exactly—or why would the plane then suddenly explode?"

"Or, what about this," said Logan. "How could a tanker full of fire retardant be ready so soon to put out the fire?"

Everyone was silent for a few moments, obviously with no answers. Finally, Finnie said, "Those are interesting questions, but right now, I'm freezing." She stood up stiffly from her concrete bench and began saying "good night" to everyone.

Li Jing concurred, "Me too Finnie. And I know we all need some sleep."

"Yep," said Logan. " Plus, I need to thaw my toes."

Reggie and Sally were each cold on one side and warm on the other from sitting in front of the fire. They also stood and said good night once again, this time to more people than before and walked across the campsite in the direction of their own tent. Though it was a little early, they were both tired, and being in the tent together was their best hope of staying warm for the night.

Chapter 50

SLIP-SLIDING AWAY

Mt. Whitney, California
November 5
5:45 p.m. (PDT)

Continuing his trek across the snowy slope parallel to the trail was awkward and difficult. Alex had to cover as much ground as possible without being seen or sliding too far downward; so, whenever he could, he used the trail directly. After the shooting incident, he had run at full tilt until he was exhausted enough to give in to a few minutes' rest before he set out again.

Best-case scenario, whoever was doing the shooting back there must think that guy with the gun is me, thought Alex. *I hope so. He looked similar enough, and no face to identify. This is the second time in three days that being considered dead has worked out well for me—at least for now until they find out I'm alive. Who knows, maybe they won't.*

Meanwhile, he had to keep going, though at a slower pace, and make it back to campsite number thirteen before his pursuers discovered that they had gotten the wrong man.

Alex resumed his previous method of walking—on the trail when he could see far enough ahead, then off the trail at other times. At this intermittent rate, he estimated another two more hours of hiking before he would reach his destination.

Off the trail, visibility ahead was limited because the trees were dense. However, this was a double-edged sword. While he could not see well ahead, the forest provided him with a degree of concealment from anyone approaching from the front who would also have the same limitation.

He was about to switch again from being off trail to rejoining it when, among the shadows of the trees about forty feet into the forest ahead, something moved.

Uh-oh, not again.

The moving object was very dark and about as big as a good-sized bear. Then, realizing that it was a bear, he froze.

Alex tried to remember what he had heard about what to do if he encountered a bear. *Okay, do I get very small and passive, or very big and badass, waving my arms?*

He decided to kneel on one knee and stay small in the hope that he would not be seen. At the same time, he remained ready to empty a whole clip of 9mm bullets into its brain and hope the animal would be a lot worse than irritated by it. However, he preferred not to shoot because of the noise it would make. Even though the snow would dampen some of the sound, he did not want to advertise his position.

Alex watched the bear carefully. It approached the trail at a perpendicular angle at first. Then it veered off to the left and back again, still moving forward, changing direction for no apparent reason. He noticed the animal was dragging its right back leg.

He thought, *Maybe it was shot in the leg. But where is the blood trail?*

Suddenly, the big bear turned to its left, as if alarmed. It roared aggressively and attacked . . . a bush. It seemed to be trying to shred it as if it were another animal; then, just as suddenly, it quit the attack, fell to the ground, and began shaking violently. It would have been a horrible sight even from a safe distance.

Alex stayed quiet until the bear was calmer and appeared to be asleep, or even dead. After the bear had not moved for six full minutes, he took a chance. Keeping in a crouched position, his finger on the trigger of the pistol, he slowly made his way onto the trail past the bear. All the while, he was watching the bear's eyes, which remained closed. He noticed a huge amount of grotesque, foamy saliva dripping from the beast's open red lips. It was all over its snout, front leg, and the snow where its leg was resting.

Disgusted, he thought to himself, *Rabies! What a news story that would make. 'Rabid Bears Found on Mount Whitney.' No one would believe it.*

Now with a new motivation—one that ignored pain and was helped by a fresh shot of adrenaline—he continued down the trail, keeping in mind that bears run faster than humans. Even so, periodically, he doubled back to cover sections of his own tracks with snow in case either man or beast was stalking him.

This was the longest short hike he had ever been on.

Chapter 51

A FEARFUL RUMOR

Mt. Whitney, California
November 5
7:30 p.m. (PDT)

At the campground, some of the people still hovered around the dwindling fire. One by one, they trailed off to bed until only Jeanie, Katie, Shen, and Li Jing were left. Nearly everyone else was either in their tent or hurriedly trying to get there because the temperature was dropping further. Sadness had settled over the group, especially Katie. Larry Gordon came over from where all the kitchen equipment was and joined them. His demeanor was equally serious.

"I need to tell you that I heard something from one of the guests tonight that did not sound good. I waited until now to mention it because, you know, I was hoping it was not accurate."

"Okay, what is it?" said Jeanie.

"The guy in site number six said he spoke with a ranger who was sure there was a shooting where someone was killed. It was over the ridge close to Meysan Lake. The person was armed and running. The description was similar. It sounds like him."

Katie stayed still, holding back tears. "Maybe I should expect the worst, but something tells me that it is not true."

"Oh, it's true all right." A voice came from out of the dark shadows. "But it wasn't me."

"Alex!" Katie cried.

He limped into the light of the fire, his feet nearly frozen.

"Alex!" repeated the others.

"Not so loud—remember, it's Shane."

"Shane!" they all said in a more subdued and unified voice.

Katie ran over and embraced and kissed him. He responded in kind, but only briefly due to the audience and the timing. She also saw that he needed medical attention.

Shen and Li Jing finally met the fugitive they were going to be harboring. All of them squeezed into one of the tents, which was just large enough with everyone sitting down. Alex, now "Shane", briefed them about what had happened in the last few hours. Meanwhile, Katie was able to treat him for frostbite on his feet and hands, as well as a place on his cheek.

"Give my apologies to the owner of that snowmobile. At least you can tell him where to find it."

Katie said, "You seem to enjoy destroying other people's property."

"I admit, I have destroyed a lot of property."

Shen pointed out the need for keeping Alex concealed. "I am imagining how your enemies may be thinking. We need to have a definite plan. I suggest that you stay as much as possible in Larry Gordon's tent. We will all get you whatever you need until it is time for everyone to pack up and go. We don't know yet when we will be able to leave, but I'm guessing tomorrow or early the next day. Clearing the road should not be that hard unless they are delaying it on purpose. Either way, you should stay inside during the daytime. We can get you into one of the cars and pack stuff around you as we get ready to go. We also need to find you another change of clothes, just in case they discover that the man they killed is not you."

Katie noticed Alex looking at Shen, then each of the others, with astonishment. After Shen had outlined his thoughts, everyone cleared out of the tent except for her and Alex.

Looking at Alex, Katie said, "What?"

"Nothing," said Alex.

"You were thinking something," She insisted.

"I'm not used to this. These people—and you—really care. I'm amazed. I've only known all of you for a few days—some for just minutes."

"Beautiful, isn't it?" she said.

"Yes, beautiful," he said, looking directly at her. "Especially you." He knew she was someone he could love quite easily from here on if he survived.

"Thank you," she replied.

"We have something powerful in common. I want to keep it if we can," he said.

"Me too. I do think you have been running, though."

"Right, like this afternoon?"

"I'm guessing for a long time, like from the One who loves you most."

"You got that right. But I won't be running from Him anymore. Even though I am on the run from certain people."

Looking at each other, they smiled and kissed until Larry complained from outside the tent, "Hey, it's cold out here—let's go."

Katie gathered up the first aid bandages and wrappers. "All right, you are good to go. You need sleep." She opened the door of the tent. "Larry, will you show Shane to his 'room' please?" she said jokingly.

Continuing the jest, Larry said, "Right this way, sir."

Larry led Alex to his tent, where a down sleeping bag and blow-up pad were ready, compliments of the California Highway Patrol's lost and found department. With his physical pain and the burden of his circumstances, Alex did not expect to get much sleep. However, when he got into the sleeping bag and rested his head on a rolled-up jacket, he felt a peace he had not experienced before. He pictured the faces of the new people in his life, who seemed committed to helping him regardless of the risk to themselves. And his thoughts kept returning to Katie.

As he drifted into a very deep sleep, instead of nightmares, he heard a familiar and melodic *fem, seks, syv, atte, ni: five, six, seven, eight, nine.*

Chapter 52

THE THIRD STORM

Mt. Whitney, California
November 5
7:30 p.m. (PDT)

Before announcing his survival to the world, the plan was for Jason to stay at the shelter for a few days or so—long enough to give the others time to escape the canyon. After dinner, he settled in for a quiet game of waiting.

Earlier that day, when Jeanie, Katie, and Alex left the shelter, a storm had been moving in. It would be the third storm of the season. Jason had gone inside the shelter and retrieved a small saw from a toolbox that was stored there. For the next hour or so, he gathered branches and arranged them against the hut so the new snow would pile up and provide better camouflage.

Back inside, his fingers were numb from exposure to the cold, and he was getting hungry. When he looked at the gauge on the propane bottle for the stove, he saw that it was nearly empty. The previous winter, he had purchased a tank top heater at Ransack's

Hardware to use on a second propane tank for the shelter. However, today, the gauge indicated that the tank was nearly empty.

Jason thought, *Looks like this should be just enough to warm up some beans and make hot cocoa, plus get my hands warm.* He was right.

Waiting and thinking go together well at times. This evening, in the quiet of the shelter, Jason realized he was missing something. For some reason, the angst—that expectation that something from out there was about to disrupt and threaten his hopes—was gone.

He thought to himself, *Man, how many times I climbed to the top of Whitney to check the horizon and settle my mind that nothing was happening.*

Then, laughing out loud, he said, "Wait a minute! It did happen! It actually happened."

That nebulous thing he feared had happened. Literally, without warning, it flew in from out there and decimated his plans and his home, swirling them together into one swift fireball. Yet he had survived. Perhaps his angst was gone now because it was no longer hypothetical. Perhaps.

For sure, Jason was still himself. But something was different about him.

I have peace, he thought. *It's not just me not worrying. This is new.*

For the last few months, Jeanie had been explaining her faith to Jason and encouraged him to commit himself to Christ by faith. He was leery of it, though, until he heard what Alex said about God being generous even if we have our back to Him. Somehow, in that moment, it had clicked, and later, he prayed to have the same relationship with God that they did. So much had happened since then, it slipped his mind.

Later that evening, he went outside with the pistol on his belt to check for visitors. A cloud-covered moon illuminated the whitened forest scape. Beauty everywhere. Jason walked over to where he could see the lake under low, hovering clouds, then back the other way as far as where they had sequestered the snowmobile when the others were there.

Before he crawled into his sleeping bag, Jason untied the laces on each of his second-hand boots, pulled them off, and put them next to the cot. For a little while, he read. Then he thought about Jeanie, and Katie, and the pilot who incinerated the coolest—or more accurately, the warmest—place he had ever lived. Weirdly, he had no hard feelings.

The stove had been off for a few hours. The temperature was dropping outside. Now snow was falling more heavily. From his cot, he reached over to the chair where his parka was and laid it across himself for extra warmth, bracing for what he expected would be a long night.

This expectation was only partly accurate. Sleep came to him right away. However, two hours later, he woke up in a sweat.

As if there was someone to address, he said out loud, "It is so hot!"

When his down bag was unzipped and the parka was on the floor, he tried again and began to doze off. Suddenly, his eyes flew open as if they were spring loaded.

"Why am I not freezing? That's a snowstorm outside."

Jason's brain was revving. He said, "Whatever made that cabin warm must be affecting this place as well. What do this place and that place have in common?"

The list of possibilities was short.

He said, "Let's see. The mountain, the forest, the altitude is about the same; me, those boots, that parka." He paused. "Those boots . . . that parka. They both came from the cabin. I have never felt cold with them on, except for my hands tonight."

Then he reached over and touched them. Neither felt especially warm. But wherever they were, the temperature was about seventy degrees, as it had always been at his cabin.

Until then, only Alex had realized that the parka and boots contained something of interest. Without knowing details, he had surmised that it was DNA from his father, and that it was at least partly what Connor was after. All of this, he had decided not to disclose to Jason. But now, Jason was putting pieces together on his own.

What if Alex's real target was not the cabin? he thought. *I'm going back in the morning. I need talk to the others.*

He did his best to get to sleep again and was so tired that he succeeded.

***

At seven the next morning, only a glimmer of light made its way into the shelter because it was covered with four feet of powdery snow; but it was still warm inside. Jason arose, took care of business, and had breakfast—corn flakes and milk that did not taste quite right, topped off with a packet of cherry Pop Tarts from the side pocket of his pack.

Out loud, he said, "Time to break silence with sis."

Texting Jeanie, he let her know he had important information to share.

She texted a reply, "Forest Service has cleared everyone to leave the canyon today. You can make the trek back now. I will wait for you at the store."

Jason texted, "How about Keven's snowmobile?"

Jeanie replied, "Not very far away but for sure unavailable—sorry. You'll have to use snowshoes. I saw some hanging at the back of the hut above the climbing ropes. What do you think will be your ETA?"

Jason replied, "Not sure with snow. Hopefully three hours or so."

Jeanie texted back, "Okay, stay warm."
Jason replied, "Definitely, I will stay warm."
Eager to get back, he started packing his gear.

Chapter 53

TIME TO GO

Mt. Whitney, California
November 6
7:00 a.m. (PDT)

An orange sun peered over the Inyo Mountain peaks, directly opposite Lone Pine Canyon. Silently, it illuminated the underside of the cloud layer that covered the entire valley, flooding all the way to the opposite end of the canyon under Mt. Whitney. Tree branches strained under the weight of new snow. Each of the red, blue, yellow, and green tents—visible in the campground the night before—looked smaller with a fresh layer of fluffy powder piled up around their edges. Officially, it was the third storm. Time to go.

More equipment had arrived from Independence at six o'clock, enough to make short work of removing the rocks and airplane parts from the road. A snowplow was parked just below the blockage, awaiting passage up to the parking areas. Logan was spreading the word from the Forest Service that the road would be clear in a little over an hour. Campers were already packing up and preparing for the slow, careful drive down the switchback road to Lone Pine.

Sleeping in a tent can be fun. Sleeping in a tent in a snowstorm can be not fun. In cold weather, having enough insulation underneath you is equally as important as having a good sleeping bag. Even then, and even inside a tent, the cold can stretch the night into a long, uncomfortable ordeal. However, Alex did not notice any of this until he finally awoke to the friendly smell of campfire smoke. A mild case of frostbite was making his toes throb.

Fortunately for him, it was breakfast in bed because he had to stay out of view as much as possible. Katie delivered a tray with coffee, bacon, Eggos and toast burned on one side. Flames leaping up from the fire had torched the bread before she could rescue it.

"Good morning, Shane. How are you feeling?" said Katie as she handed the tray to him through the opening. Then moving through it into the tent, she sat cross-legged on the floor.

"I feel alive now that you are here," said Alex.

She laughed.

Peering out through the mesh window of the tent, he said, "It looks like it snowed pretty heavily."

"Yes, last night was the third storm of the season. Normally that's the signal for the Forest Service to close the canyon, but I guess you beat them to it by landing part of your airplane on the road," she said jokingly.

"Yeah, that was a close call," said Alex.

"Well, I just learned that the road will be officially open in about an hour. A snowplow is clearing it now and we can start packing up. We have a plan to get you out of here," said Katie.

When Alex heard the words We have a plan, he became alarmed by a disturbing thought: *Wait, I'm about to trust people I do not know well—civilians even—with my life!* Emotionally, he was yanked from the comfort he had been enjoying with Katie back to the way he had conducted his life before parachuting from his plane. As a natural leader and tactician, he was accustomed to being in charge. In combat, he was the one who decided the next move. For the moment, he seemed to have lost the clarity and trust that he'd felt the last few days since he met Jason and the others. Katie had a disarming effect on him, and "Savage One" was not used to being disarmed.

"Who is 'we?'" Alex asked.

Somewhat stunned, Katie answered, "Well . . . the pastor and his wife, and Larry, and the couple in the RV, Logan and Sheri. They are the official campground hosts. Also, Jeanie and me," she said.

"What is an 'official' campground host? What keeps them from handing me over to other 'officials?'" he asked.

"Didn't they just hide you in their camp all night? We told them the whole situation and they got it. None of them are naïve. They can tell when something is not right. In fact, Shen and Li Jing know what it is like to run from their own government."

"Oh," said Alex, still struggling with his natural instinct. "What about Larry, isn't he a detective or something?" asked Alex.

"Yes, but before he got his act together, he was on the other side of the law. He is confident this is the best thing to do," she said, getting annoyed. "You will just have to start living dangerously, Colonel, and trust us. Besides, how do you know you can trust me? I could turn you in if I wanted to."

"You won't," he said.

"How do you know?" she said.

"I'm a good judge of character."

"Really," she said sarcastically, laughing.

"Really."

"All right, here is the plan," said Katie emphatically. "You will be going with Logan and Sheri in their RV. We're going to pack you up in the upper bunk under all the bedding. They will take you as far as Bishop or Mammoth, depending on what your plan is going to be."

Alex interrupted, "Hold on. So, I get that this older couple is trying to help, but they don't deserve this kind of danger. If I'm discovered, there will be a gunfight. These agents tried to kill me twice already. It will be too dangerous."

"You are a stubborn man!" she replied.

"No, I'm not," he said stubbornly. "Look, I am grateful for all this, but I think I should go down alone in a borrowed car and leave it somewhere it can be picked up."

"The way you take care of other people's stuff, if you borrow someone's car, they can kiss it goodbye!" she said.

"You seem to have a little mean streak. Hey, are you crying?"

"No!" she said, wiping tears from her cheek. "I just prefer that you stay alive, that's all."

"That's all?" he asked.

"No," she said. "Think of the close calls you had yesterday, and the day before, and who knows how many other times—you don't think it was you that saved your own life do you? You know who it was! Now, even pieces of your own airplane are spread all over this canyon, but here you are, safe—and doubting everyone who is on your side!"

"Oh. Okay," he replied. "I'm sorry. I was just hit with some doubts and switched over to how I did things when I was alone."

"Alex, they think—"

"Shane."

"Shane, they think you are dead. You said the guy they shot was dressed the same as you were, and his face was destroyed. They are not looking for you anymore. All you need to do is stay out of the public eye just in case," said Katie.

"All right. I've made some bad decisions lately," said Alex, "so one more might not matter. But first, I want to talk with Kuan about it, then the host."

"Okay, I'll tell them to come by your tent, but it will have to be soon. Everyone is breaking camp. We plan to be the last ones to leave, so you have to make it over to Logan's RV unnoticed. Be sure to wear the hoodie, then just carry a big pile of blankets and pillows into the RV as if you are helping Logan and Sheri. That will help obscure your face. Once you are in the RV, stay there."

She continued, "So, what is your plan beyond this? What do you need?"

"I need to learn what this whole DNA thing is about and why they are trying to kill me," he said. "And I need to know what the hell this weapon is and put a stop to it if I can. In my mind, I keep hearing part of a counting song from five to nine. It matches a memory I have of nine granite steps leading to Jason's cabin. My father cut those steps into the boulder when he built it."

"You hear numbers?" she asked.

"Yes, but in Norwegian. I hear the song in Norwegian. After I lay low for long enough to see if anyone is still hunting me, I'm going over there to see what I can learn about my father and whatever he was working on before he died."

"You're going to Norway?"

"Yes, and after that I'm going to find Connor. He and I are going to have a little talk."

"Okay," said Katie. "We have all been discussing this and agree that we want to be available to help with what you are doing. Jason too. He sent Jeanie a text this morning. He is hiking all the way back on snowshoes today and he wants in on whatever it is," she said.

Alex was finally convinced. He thought, *During the short time they have been together, these people seem to have a nearly instant connection—as if something greater has drawn them together.*

Right then, Shen appeared at the doorway of the tent.

"May I come in?" he asked.

"Please," both of them replied.

Shen stooped down to enter the tent and sat across from Alex and Katie.

Alex addressed him. "Mr. Kuan, thank you for accommodating me in my unusual situation. I do not take it lightly."

"You are welcome, Shane," he said. "What is your plan? How can we help?"

"Katie and I were just discussing this. But first, let me ask you: why are you risking so much to help me? You know it will cost you a lot if the authorities learn what you have done."

"True. However, your situation feels very familiar to me, and I think it is the right thing to do. As a Christian, I'm trusting God for how it goes," Shen replied.

"Fair enough," Alex said. "Okay, the first order of business is for me to get away from here, then blend in for a while. I'm thinking there are plenty of hikers around here. If I can borrow one of Larry's sleeping bags and a backpack, I can take day jobs for cash and get a cheap hotel up the road, maybe in Bishop. I'll need to get a new identity somehow, and a plane ticket out of the country—Norway. Eventually, I hope to pay a visit to an ex-friend who I believe is behind all this."

Shen said, "We all knew you would be wanting to do something about whatever is behind the scenes, so we've decided to pay your way."

"What?" replied Alex.

Shen handed him a roll of cash and said, "We all came up with enough for some food and a place to stay, so we'll start there. Katie will be our contact with you. I suggest that you speak only with her for now. By the way, if you have credit cards, be sure not to use them, no matter what, or you will be discovered. And Larry pointed out that if you are going to investigate these things you will need a computer, so he is going to provide a laptop for you. He is an amateur tech guy. He will make it reasonably secure so internet activity will not be traced to you." Then, jokingly, he added, "I understand you are dead. Is that correct?"

Getting the joke and feeling honored by the gift, Alex said, "Yes, that's right."

"My sympathies."

"Thanks."

Shen and Katie exited the tent and continued helping the other campers pack. Alex sat alone on the sleeping bag, legs crossed. The frostbite on his toes felt sore but significantly improved. Though he knew the days ahead would be difficult, he was grateful for the new friends who had seemed to appear out of thin air. But then, he had appeared to them out of thin air first—in a more literal way.

***

For Reggie and Sally, the cold had made the night longer as they waited for the warmth of the morning. But when it finally came, it was not as warm as they had hoped. Both were preferring their chilly bedding to the frosty air when they heard the voice of Li Jing calling to them from outside their tent.

Li Jing said, "Good morning, Sally. Good morning, Reggie. I brought some good news—and breakfast."

Opening the entrance flap, Sally said, "Breakfast? Li Jing, this is wonderful! I was dreading the thought of having to make something. Thank you so much."

Reggie echoed her gratitude and asked, "What is the good news?"

"Just now, the road has been cleared. We are free to go," said Li

Jing. "Enjoy your breakfast." She walked off. The warm food was a great relief.

"Reggie," Sally said, "I feel these people are our friends. They are so kind."

"I expected them to cut us off when we didn't see the universe the way they did. I guess it was me that cut them off. I'm glad we stayed with them. They are real, aren't they?"

After eating, they both went over to the other campsite to return the dishes and say goodbye to the others. They even exchanged contact information. Shen and Li Jing invited them to call if they ever wanted to and suggested that they meet for dinner sometime.

On the way back to their camp on the snow-covered road, they saw Logan and Sheri and went over to bid them farewell. Sally noticed a guy with a hoodie carrying a very big load of blankets to Logan's RV and wondered if he could see where he was going as he plodded through the thick snow. She felt there was something familiar about him but dismissed the thought.

Logan said, "Reggie, Sally, I have enjoyed your company. On top of that, I have a special respect for you because of the profession you chose since it is all about reporting the truth. I don't know what you're going to write about all those rabid bears—but with you two, I'm sure it will be the truth."

Sally smiled. "Thank you, Logan. We've enjoyed your company as well."

Reggie added, "Oh, yeah. Thanks. And we are definitely glad we got the official word to switch assignments since that jet crashed into our mountain."

"That's good because your other story was going to be a dud," said Logan.

They all laughed.

"Also," Logan continued, "Sheri and I hope you both consider what the pastor was saying about trusting Christ in a personal way. If it's true, which we I believe it is, then you have a lot to gain by it."

"Thank you, Logan. You have given me a different perspective than I had. I'm glad we could all just talk about it rather than argue," Sally said. Reggie nodded.

"Just so you know, you can ask Jesus to be your Lord any time or place. It may be scary because He wants us to turn over every part of our lives. But He makes it well worth it."

"I admit that idea is scary," said Sally, "but since you are so sure, at least, I promise to consider seriously what you are saying."

"Me too," said Reggie. "Thanks."

Logan added, "By the way, I have a tip for you. It could be a great story. I think you mentioned that you met the guy who owned the cabin that got blown up, right?"

"Yes. It's such a shame because he was really a nice guy," she said.

"Well, his sister, Jeanie, told me he is alive. When it happened, he was across the mountain. She says he will be hiking back today and will be meeting her at the store up the hill in a few hours. If you want to go up there, you may be able to find them."

"What?! This is great news! Yes, we will follow up," she said.

"Meanwhile, have a nice trip home," said Logan.

"You too," said Reggie.

Chapter 54

HOMEWARD BOUND

Mt. Whitney, California
November 6
9:30 a.m. (PDT)

Black ice made the ride down the mountain slow-going for everyone. After most of the people from the campsites and cabins had left the Portal, Shen and Li Jing followed the members of their group down the mountain. Then, Logan and Sheri started down in the RV, with Alex stuffed into the top forward bunk with a lot of bedding around him for concealment. In that position, he was able to see ahead through a rectangular window in the front.

Looking out, one of the first sights Alex encountered was the left wing of his aircraft, lying on the shoulder of the road where it had been pushed aside with the rest of the rubble. Still visible through the scorched paint was the United States Air Force insignia. Sobering, angering, reminiscent of Connor's betrayal, it represented the wreckage of his career and his reputation. Although flying was what he loved, and what he did for his country, as far as he knew, Alex might never fly again.

About a mile later, as they passed the Vista Point pullout just before the road steepened, Alex's heart began to race. A green truck with a U.S. Forest Service emblem on the door was waiting to enter the roadway. Inside the cab, a man and woman dressed in green uniforms were talking to each other. One was the pretty and familiar face of the agent who had killed him—or thought she had—the day before. Instinctively, his thumb found the safety on his pistol and released it.

All the way down the mountain, tension was high as the green truck followed directly behind the RV. Alex remained ready for a showdown, at the same time regretting that he had let himself go along with the plan for him to ride with Logan and Sheri.

He called to Logan with as calm a voice as he could so as not to alarm them: "Hey, Logan, keep your eye on that green truck behind us. If they stop us, I'm going through this window, so when I do, you and Sheri get down on the floor."

Logan replied, "No problem, Colonel, I've already been watching them. They've been talking and laughing. Looks like they are just sightseeing now."

When they finally reached Lone Pine, Logan turned in at the Chevron station. To their dismay, the green truck followed all the way in and parked on their right side, across from the pumps. The male "ranger" got out and went inside the store, evidently to use the facilities. Logan got out and began filling the tank, while Sheri went inside, ostensibly for snacks and to pay for the gas. Meanwhile, she kept an eye on the man inside. In the checkout line, the man let her go in front of him.

She noticed the gun on his hip and, half-joking, she asked, "When was the last time you had to use that pistol?"

"Oh—well, unfortunately, just yesterday. It was sad, though. He was a good guy that went bad. But it had to be done."

"I'm sorry to hear that. Have a good day."

"Thank you, ma'am," he replied.

Back in the RV, Sheri reported the interaction. "It looks like they are sure you are out of the picture."

Alex said, "Okay, but time will tell if they change their minds or not."

When they pulled out of the gas station and turned toward Bishop, it was a relief to see the green truck headed in the other direction, toward Ridgecrest and China Lake.

"Bishop is forty-two miles up the road past the town of Independence.", Sheri said, as she pulled out her phone. "Searching online for a hotel for your situation, will be a lot easier than finding one for a vacation." After a few minutes, she continued, "Oh, this one looks good; run-down, inexpensive, low ratings and, looks like low visibility off the main road. A single reservation for an open-ended stay is all you need."

"Good," said Logan, "We'll let Larry know where you are. Later tonight, he'll bring you a computer and a burner phone. Larry said to meet him at Jed's Coffee Shop. Looks like it's up the street from the hotel. He thinks it will be safer if you meet after dark, about seven. Larry also suggested that you start growing a beard and try to look older, maybe get some gray hair coloring."

"Already doing that, thanks," said Alex. "Tell him I'll be at Jed's at seven tonight. Also, to remember my name is Shane now."

"Okay. Katie should show up there too," said Sheri. "She will be your main contact."

"Logan, Sheri, thank you," said Alex.

"No problem. We get it. Sheri and I are going over from here to stay at the Ski Resort in Mammoth. We'll be in touch with Katie and available if you need anything. For now, though, just lay low."

***

About thirty minutes after Logan and Sheri left the Portal area, Larry started down the road. As soon as he arrived at home, he got busy in his workshop. Larry's friends described him as, "a geek at heart." He had a lot of computers, and a lot of knowledge. Before long, he had a laptop ready to go for Alex.

Meanwhile, Katie decided to wait with Jeanie to make sure Jason made it back safely.

At about one o'clock, Jason arrived. Jeanie was especially glad to see her brother. She greeted him with a fresh coffee from the Portal store.

As they were sitting on a bench by the frozen pond, Jason heard a familiar voice: "Excuse me, Jason. Remember us? Sally Rogers and Reggie Willard."

Pleasantly surprised, Jason replied, "Of course, Sally and Reggie from just a few days ago. Hello again."

Reggie said, "We're so glad to see that you are safe."

"Yes, what a relief," added Sally.

"For us too," said Jeanie. Katie nodded in agreement.

Sally said, "Jason, we know you must be exhausted, but do you think we could do a very short interview for a news story? By now, practically the whole world will be happy to hear that you are back with us."

Jason, replied, "Sure, I could do that, but for now I don't really want it to be on video."

"I fully understand," said Sally. "Whatever you are willing to do is okay."

Katie and Jeanie stood up and offered Sally their place and she sat down next to Jason on the bench.

Jason explained how he happened to be away from his cabin the night of the incident, alluding vaguely to finding a safe place to stay. Of course, he did not include the part about meeting the person who destroyed his home.

"You seem calm and peaceful, even after losing that beautiful cabin," Sally said. "Do you normally take a loss like this so calmly?"

Jason replied, "I had some time to think about things up there, but I guess it is still kind of new. It is just great to be alive."

"Well, I am certainly glad you made it through this alive, Jason. Welcome back. Would you mind if we follow up with you in the future?" she asked.

"Sure, any time," he said.

During the interview, Sally was exuding an extra enthusiasm—it seemed to Jason more personal than business. At times her eyes were wide with interest in his story, then she would turn away suddenly to her notes as if she were trying to rein herself in. As a caring person, she was obviously happy to see him alive. *But* he thought, *she seems pretty alive too.*

Jason tried not to be too obvious about how much he was attracted to her. He wondered—hoped—that she was doing the same thing. He was not sure if he was reading her accurately or not. But, since their present focus was only on the interview, he determined that he would find a way to contact her in the future.

Katie said, "Jason, let's go over here to the Portal store and get you something to eat."

With an exchange of friendly goodbyes, they started off in that direction. After walking a few yards, Jason stopped and turned back. He approached Sally and said, "Hey, I'd like to take you to lunch sometime. This time maybe I could interview you. I'm sure it would be interesting. Can I get your number?"

Jason saw her eyes sparkle for a moment as she realized what he was asking.

She smiled and said, "Okay, yes. I think I would like that." She reached into her purse, pulled out a business card, and gave it to him.

"Good, I'll call you in a week or so, after I take care of some things."

With that, Jason turned and set out to catch up with Jeanie and Katie. Reggie and Sally began setting up their video equipment by the pond to make their own mobile news video.

Normally, the Portal store and pond area teemed with people—often from different parts of the world. Today, only two customers were at the store, both young men. They were sitting at a table outside, eating. The parking lot was emptying. People were finally headed home. Jason and the two women walked by the tables.

One of the young men said to the other, "The guy inside, Greg, told me these were the last hamburgers of the season. He said it was because of 'the third storm.' All I could think of was Jason telling us about winter. I can't believe he didn't make it out alive."

Jason, standing right next to their table and listening in, said loudly, "Sounds like a rumor to me."

Chet and Nate looked up at Jason, mouths open, astonished. Great smiles formed on their happy faces. Both jumped up with one motion, crying out, "Jason!" Nate absentmindedly put his full weight on his injured foot and shouted, "Ow!"

"We thought you were a goner. It was horrible!" said Chet.

"Well, you should always be away from home when your house blows up," said Jason.

Jeanie and Katie watched the mini celebration with amusement, remembering the way they discovered that Alex had survived the night before. Meanwhile, Jason explained how he had met Chet and Nate in the summer, then again on the trail a few days earlier.

Katie said, "Actually, I met Nate and Chet too, a couple of days ago. They were in the campsite across the road from ours."

Nate said, "Thanks for helping with my foot. Packing it with snow helped."

"And for inviting us for dinner," added Chet.

"You're welcome," answered Katie. "I'm glad your ankle feels better but be sure to see a doctor about it when you get home."

"And we do need to get out of here before the road freezes again," said Chet.

"I guess there won't be a warm place up here now that your cabin is gone," said Nate.

Jeanie and Katie gave Jason a startled look, not liking that the boys knew about the cabin.

"Yeah, that's right," Jason said. "Do me a favor, though. Now that it is gone, let's keep that info about the cabin between you and me, okay?"

"Sure, you bet, Jason," they said.

"Hey, have a safe trip back, you guys," said Jason.

When Jeanie, Katie, and Jason were alone again, they brought Jason up to speed about their plans. Jason had insights to share as well as they made their way down to Lone Pine, where Dale was waiting for them at home. Jason would be staying in their casita once again, at least until he could discern what to do next. He only knew it would have something to do with a pilot friend who was on the run.

Chapter 55

UNEXPECTED SURVIVOR

Bishop, California
November 6
6:00 p.m. (PDT)

Rose McPherson, news anchor, introduced the evening report.

"Good evening. Tonight, we have unexpected, good news. Just a few days ago, the world was shocked and perplexed by violent explosions at Mt. Whitney. A rogue fighter pilot fired a missile randomly at a cabin, destroying it instantly. Authorities were certain that the cabin's owner, forest ranger Jason Greer, had been killed in the blast. However, we have learned that earlier this afternoon, Mr. Greer reappeared. Reporters Sally Rogers and Reggie Willard from our affiliate, Independence News, have this story."

The video switched to a feed from the Mt. Whitney Portal Campground with a snow-covered pond in the background. Sally and Reggie were standing side by side and smiling into a camera on a tripod in front of them.

Rose said, "Sally and Reggie, great job staying so close to this story. What can we learn about Mr. Greer? Where has he been?"

Sally took the lead, "Thank you, Rose. Indeed, it has been a tumultuous time in this otherwise peaceful mountain resort. Many people were mourning the apparent loss of U.S. Forest Service ranger Jason Greer when his residence was suddenly destroyed in the middle of the night by, of all things, a missile from an Air Force jet. Subsequently, the pilot died when his fighter jet crashed and exploded, and we all thought Mr. Greer was a tragic second casualty. However, today, we were happy to learn, that at the time of the incident, Ranger Greer was not at home."

She turned to Reggie, who continued, "That's right. This afternoon around one o'clock, he showed up at the general store after hiking in on snowshoes from a different canyon. Greer preferred not to do an interview on camera, but we did speak with him and his sister. While, of course, there was sadness over the loss of his home, they both celebrated his surviving the ordeal."

Sally added, "Interestingly, though he had been hiking all morning in freezing temperatures, he told us that he rarely feels the cold. In his words, 'It's all about having the right clothes.'"

Rose laughed. "Not me. No matter what I wear in the snow, I come back frozen."

"Me too," said Sally. "Mr. Greer's sister, Jeanie, commented that 'somebody up there' must have been looking out for her brother, because just a few hours before the incident, he set out on a trek into the Inyo wilderness to check for hikers who may have been in trouble, narrowly missing the devastating explosion."

Reggie added, "As a sidenote, Rose, Sally and I were here working on a different assignment the day before the incident, and we happened to interview Mr. Greer at the very cabin which is, of course, no longer there."

"Since we had met him before, it was a great relief to learn that he survived," said Sally.

Rose concluded, "Sally Rogers and Reggie Willard from the Mt. Whitney Portal Campground. Thank you both ."

Chapter 56

POWER BROKERS

Abu Dhabi, United Arab Emirates
November 7
5:35 p.m. (GST)

"How's your English these days, brother?!"

Cheerful, welcoming, the voice called out across the sand to a man standing barefoot on the beach in front of the Emirates Palace Mandarin Oriental hotel. Except for his feet, he was dressed in business attire; dark blue suit, white shirt, and tie. In his left hand, he held a pair of black sandals. The man had been watching a very large orange sun kiss the far horizon of the Persian Gulf and begin merging with the sea. He was captivated.

At the sound of the greeting, Kasym Nazarov broke from his trance and turned to see his old friend, Rami ibn Faheem. Light from the setting sun tinted Faheem's long, white cotton kandura to orange, as it did the beach and surrounding buildings. His traditional white ghutra headdress was held in place by a black agal. Two cords ending in tassels dangled at the back. As a member of the government, he was also in business attire.

"Rami!" said Nazarov with a smile.

"Kasym!" he replied.

Both men hugged lightly and kissed each other on both cheeks.

"It is so good to see you in person, my friend," said Nazarov.

"And you, but you have gotten so old!" joked Faheem.

"You forgot to say, 'but wise,'" said Nazarov.

"That's right and wise is better than young!" he replied.

"Well, maybe . . ." both men laughed.

"London seems so long ago," said Nazarov. "Do you know if the language school is still there?"

"Yes, but they have given it a longer name, 'The London School of International Communication.'" Mohammed bin Salman attended there as well. And did you know that the Sheik was mentor to Salman when he was younger?"

"Yes, and Rami, thank you for speaking to His Highness. It is very important that we meet."

"Of course, but you owe me, Kasym, especially since you say I am not allowed to know what you will tell him. You are sure about that?" he asked.

"Unfortunately, yes, or as the Americans say, 'Or else I would have to . . .,'" he said.

"Fine, fine, I see that you are still stubborn," said Faheem. "I will know what it is only if the Sheikh decides to tell me."

"And perhaps he will," said Nazarov.

"All right, the Shiekh is in the council now. Today it is a meeting with a group of deputy rulers. Any time now, they will have a short break, and he will come out. You will have only a few minutes to speak with him unless he decides to give you more time. See that palm at the edge of the pool there?," said Faheem, pointing. "Wait there. I will walk over to you with him and introduce you. Then I will leave you to speak with each other."

"I understand," said Nazarov.

"And Kasym, I suggest you put your sandals on," he said with a smile and walked off toward the hotel.

Nazarov walked to the sidewalk alongside the pool. He shook the sand from his feet, put on his sandals, and took his place beside the palm tree. A warm breeze from the beach shuffled the fronds above him slightly as he waited.

Soon, the double doors to the meeting room opened to the outside. Men, about eight or so, all dressed in similar white kanduras and headdresses came out, some laughing, others locked in serious discussion. Nearly every man sported a carefully trimmed black beard.

Among those emerging from the building was Rami Faheem. He was talking with a taller man. As they walked along, he gestured toward the palm tree by the pool where Nazarov was standing, and they turned in that direction. As they approached, Faheem stepped forward to introduce the two men.

"Your Highness," he said, "I would like you to meet a fellow student and friend from long ago, Kasym Nazarov."

"Rami you are so formal," said the Crowned Prince with a friendly tone. To Nazarov, he said, "If Rami is your friend, you have been blessed."

As the two men exchanged greetings, the Sheikh was cordial yet reserved.

Then Faheem said, "I know you both have something to discuss so I will leave you."

"Thank you, Rami," said the Sheikh.

Faheem walked back toward the meeting room doors and stood

near a large planter with pink and white flowers. Because he expected it to be a short conversation, he remained ready to rejoin his superior and accompany him back to the meeting. However, after a few minutes, Faheem saw the two of them walk off together onto the beach as if to find more privacy. The Sheik seemed to be listening intently. Faheem noticed that whenever the Sheikh spoke, he gestured with his hands as he typically did when he was asking questions.

Time stretched on. The other leaders had returned to the meeting room. His Highness had indeed given Nazarov more time, apparently with great interest. Though Faheem could not hear them, the two men spoke of their common aspirations and what it might take to fulfill them. Both were power brokers, doing what they did best.

Daylight faded. Only solitary stars illuminated the night sky.

TO BE CONTINUED